Comma

"Very well," the man

all here. Let's get started. Henry Irving and Ellen Terry have arrived in New York. They have already performed this evening."

"Why were they allowed to perform?" one man asked. "That was not the plan."

"Plans change," said the man at the head of the table. "Mr. Gray?"

The man who had arrived late—and whose name was not "Mr. Gray"—said, "The United States government has assigned them a bodyguard."

"That was expected," someone said.

"In fact," another man said, "it was assumed."

"Mr. White and Mr. Green are both correct," Mr. Gray said. "However, there was no way we could anticipate who that person would be."

"We assumed they would want to assign their best man," the man at the head of the table said. "We took steps to have James West assigned elsewhere."

"According to plan," Mr. Green pointed out.

"Yes, but what happened next was not according to plan," Mr. Gray said.

"Well," Mr. Red said, "don't keep us in suspense. Who is the bodyguard?"

"His name is Clint Adams," Mr. Gray said.

Silence fell over the table as the men exchanged glances.

"The Gunsmith," Mr. Yellow said.

DON'T MISS THESE ALL-ACTION WESTERN SERIES FROM THE BERKLEY PUBLISHING GROUP

THE GUNSMITH by J. R. Roberts

Clint Adams was a legend among lawmen, outlaws, and ladies. They called him . . . the Gunsmith.

LONGARM by Tabor Evans

The popular long-running series about Deputy U.S. Marshal Custis Long—his life, his loves, his fight for justice.

SLOCUM by Jake Logan

Today's longest-running action Western. John Slocum rides a deadly trail of hot blood and cold steel.

BUSHWHACKERS by B. J. Lanagan

An action-packed series by the creators of Longarm! The rousing adventures of the most brutal gang of cutthroats ever assembled—Quantrill's Raiders.

DIAMONDBACK by Guy Brewer

Dex Yancey is Diamondback, a Southern gentleman turned con man when his brother cheats him out of the family fortune. Ladies love him. Gamblers hate him. But nobody pulls one over on Dex . . .

WILDGUN by Jack Hanson

The blazing adventures of mountain man Will Barlow—from the creators of Longarm!

TEXAS TRACKER by Tom Calhoun

J.T. Law: the most relentless—and dangerous—manhunter in all Texas. Where sheriffs and posses fail, he's the best man to bring in the most vicious outlaws—for a price.

J. R. ROBERTS

JOVE BOOKS, NEW YORK

THE BERKLEY PUBLISHING GROUP
Published by the Penguin Group
Penguin Group (USA) Inc.
375 Hudson Street, New York, New York 10014, USA
Penguin Group (Canada), 90 Eglinton Avenue East, Suite 700, Toronto, Ontario M4P 2Y3, Canada (a division of Pearson Penguin Canada Inc.) • Penguin Books Ltd., 80 Strand, London WC2R 0RL, England • Penguin Group Ireland, 25 St. Stephen's Green, Dublin 2, Ireland (a division of Penguin Books Ltd.) • Penguin Group (Australia), 250 Camberwell Road, Camberwell, Victoria 3124, Australia (a division of Pearson Australia Group Pty. Ltd.) • Penguin Books India Pvt. Ltd., 11 Community Centre, Panchsheel Park, New Delhi—110 017, India • Penguin Group (NZ), 67 Apollo Drive, Rosedale, Auckland 0632, New Zealand (a division of Pearson New Zealand Ltd.) • Penguin Books (South Africa) (Pty.) Ltd., 24 Sturdee Avenue, Rosebank, Johannesburg 2196, South Africa

Penguin Books Ltd., Registered Offices: 80 Strand, London WC2R 0RL, England

FRATERNITY OF THE GUN

A Jove Book / published by arrangement with the author

PUBLISHING HISTORY
Jove edition / October 2012

ISBN: 978-0-515-15114-5

JOVE®
Jove Books are published by The Berkley Publishing Group,
a division of Penguin Group (USA) Inc.,
375 Hudson Street, New York, New York 10014.
JOVE® is a registered trademark of Penguin Group (USA) Inc.
The "J" design is a trademark of Penguin Group (USA) Inc.

PRINTED IN THE UNITED STATES OF AMERICA

10 9 8 7 6 5 4 3 2 1

ONE

Clint Adams spread the cards in his hand and kept his face bland as he studied them. Across the table the only other player in the hand, Beau Grant, was eyeing his own cards, and sweating. Perhaps the worse tell of all to have for a poker player was the inability to control his own sweat.

"Well?" Clint asked. "It's your bet."

Grant was in his thirties, but he still lived in a house with his mother and father. He played poker with his father's money.

"A hundred," Grant said, tossing the money into the already substantial pot.

"That's not much of a bet," Clint said. "You opened the betting, and you drew two cards. Your draw was only worth a hundred? Or are you betting on your original three of a kind?"

"You can't know that I had three of a kind," Grant said.

"Lucky guess," Clint said. "Here's your hundred, and another five."

"You're bluffing," Grant said. Sweat dripped from the point of his chin onto the green felt of the table. Clint looked past him, saw a tall man in an expensive suit enter the gambling hall. The man walked to the bar and spoke to the bartender, who inclined his head Clint's way. The tall man looked over and nodded. Then he asked for a beer.

Clint looked back at Grant.

"Five hundred more," he repeated.

"Bluffing," Grant said, but more to himself than to anyone else.

"It will cost you five hundred to find out," Clint said. "That is, unless you want to raise."

The three other players at the table were watching, and smiling. They had been waiting days for someone to take down Beau Grant. When Clint had walked in earlier that day and joined the game, somehow they knew it would be him.

"I—I call," Grant said. Then he threw down his cards. "Kings full of threes," he said.

"He drew two threes to three kings," one of the other players said. "What luck."

"Adams drew three cards," one of the other players said. "Let's see what he drew."

"I had two jacks . . ." Clint said, putting two black Jacks on the table.

"Hah!" Grant said, reaching for the chips.

"And I drew two more." He put two red jacks next to the black.

"Four jacks," one of the other players said.

"Great hand!" another said.

"He busted the kid," the third player said.

Grant just stared across the table at Clint, then abruptly stood and stormed out of the saloon.

Clint collected his chips, and accepted the congratulations and backslaps of the other players.

"Any more takers?" Clint asked.

"Nope," one of the players said. "We're done. Mr. Adams. It's been a pleasure."

They all stood and walked to the bar.

The tall man from the bar approached with two beers, set one down on the table in front of Clint.

"Mr. Adams?"

"That's what the bartender told you, isn't it?" Clint asked.

"Yes, sir. May I sit?"

"I'll only be here as long as it takes to count my chips and cash in."

"Perhaps that's all the time I'll need," the man said.

"Then sit."

As the man sat down, Clint picked up the beer and drank half of it down. Poker was hard work, and he didn't drink while he played.

"Thanks for the beer," he said.

"My name is Allan Trehearn."

"Mr. Trehearn," Clint said. "What brings you to New Orleans?"

"You do," Trehearn said. "I came here looking for you."

"What for?"

"I have a request to ask of you."

"I don't usually hear requests from strangers," Clint

said. That was true. He was too busy fielding requests from friends.

"Then perhaps I should tell you who sent me," Trehearn said.

Clint finished stacking his chips and said, "Maybe you should."

"A man named Jim West."

Clint stared at Trehearn.

TWO

Clint cashed in his chips, then walked with Trehearn back to the bar. There they each got a fresh beer.

"Okay," Clint said. "Since you have Jim West's name, I'll listen to you. What's it about?"

"The Department of State was contacted by the British government. Apparently two of their citizens are coming to the United States on tour."

"On tour?"

"They're actors," Trehearn said. "Well, an actor and an actress. Henry Irving and Ellen Terry."

"I never heard of them."

"Well, they're pretty famous over there," Trehearn said.

"Okay, so what does this have to do with me?" Clint asked.

"They need a bodyguard," Trehearn said. "They're going to stop at some of the top theaters in our country and perform."

"What part of the country?"

"All of it," Trehearn said. "East to west, starting in New York."

"You want me to recommend a bodyguard?"

"No," Trehearn said, "State wants you to be the bodyguard."

"Why me?"

"Because," Trehearn said, "West recommended you."

"Why would he do that?"

"Because he was going to be their bodyguard, but something else came up. Something—"

"Don't tell me, of national importance."

"International," Trehearn said. "So he's going to be out of the country. State was going to assign another man, but they couldn't decide on who it should be until West mentioned you."

Clint cursed to himself. Jim West was one of his best friends. He had never turned down a request from him, or a job that West had recommended him for.

"What do you say?" Trehearn asked.

"When will they be in New York?"

"They should be arriving next week," Trehearn said. "We can supply a private train to take you there."

Clint took a moment to drink some beer and think.

"You can leave tomorrow," Trehearn added.

"I have . . . other obligations here," Clint said.

"This important?"

"Perhaps not to you, or State," Clint said, "but to me."

"So then when can you leave?"

"I haven't accepted this job yet."

"What more do you need to know?"

"Well, for one thing," Clint said, "is it a job? Am I being paid?"

"You're being asked to perform a service for your country."

"As a bodyguard to an actor and an actress?" Clint asked.

"We don't need an international incident," Trehearn said. "These people are very important to the British. They are apparently both considered national treasures. We need to ensure their safety every moment they're here."

"And they won't be here for a week?"

"At least."

"Okay," Clint said.

"Okay . . . what?" Trehearn asked.

"Okay, I'll do it."

"When can you leave?"

"Tomorrow afternoon."

"When tomorrow afternoon?" Trehearn asked. "The sooner the better, Mr. Adams."

"Noon," Clint said. "I'll be ready at noon."

"No earlier?"

"I have some loose ends to tie up," Clint said. "But I'll be ready at noon."

"All right," Trehearn said, clearly unhappy. "I'll telegraph Washington and let them know. And there will be a ticket waiting for you at the station."

"What about you?"

"What about me?" Trehearn asked.

"Are you going to be along on this little job?"

"No, I can't," Trehearn said. "But I'll be your contact

in State. You'll be able to contact me at any time by telegraph."

"What about supplies?"

"Anything you need," Trehearn said. "You'll have carte blanche."

"*Anything* I need?"

"Anything," Trehearn said, "within reason."

"What does that mean?"

"I guess we'll find that out when the time comes," Trehearn said.

THREE

After they went over some details—most notably, expenses—Clint went up to his room. He had been in New Orleans for three days. The Lafitte Hotel and Gambling Hall was just outside the French Quarter. He had come there not to help anybody with their problem, not to hunt anybody, just to have some time to himself—with some gambling and women tossed in.

Instead, it had become some gambling and *one* woman. Her name was Charlotte Temple, and she was waiting for him in his room. They had spent the previous two nights together, and this would be their third—and last.

When he entered his room, she was still naked in his bed.

"Did you win?" she asked.

"I did," he said.

"Well," she said, getting to her knees, "you're about to win some more."

He had intended to tell her that he was leaving the next day, but he decided that could wait awhile . . .

Allan Trehearn left the Lafitte and walked a few blocks into the French Quarter. When he came to the Napoleon House Saloon, he stepped inside and took a look around. The Napoleon was small, but well furnished, a place people went to drink in peace and silence, with no gambling going on.

Seated at a back table, he saw his man and walked over. He was tall, slender, bald, well dressed in a suit even more expensive than Trehearn's. He was in his forties, and had an air of complete confidence about him.

"Get us two brandies, will you?" the man asked.

"Sure."

Trehearn walked to the bar, bought two brandies, and returned to the table.

"Thanks," the other man said. He finished the brandy he had, set the empty glass down, and accepted the new one from Trehearn. "Have a seat."

Trehearn sat down opposite the man and looked around. There were only four other people in the place, and none of them were paying them any attention.

"Did he bite?" the man asked.

"Yes," Trehearn said. "He's going tomorrow at noon."

"On the government train?"

"Right."

"Good," the other man said. "That was easier than I thought."

"I told you all we had to do was invoke the name 'Jim West.' "

"And what about West?" the man asked. "Where is he really?"

"He really is out of the country," Trehearn said. "That's what makes this work."

"All right," the man said. "Tomorrow Clint Adams will be on his way to New York."

"Yes."

"And you are on your way to . . ."

"Philadelphia is my next stop," Trehearn said.

"Right."

The man sipped his brandy.

"And where will you be?" Trehearn asked.

"There's a saloon in Philadelphia called the Delphi," the man said. "I'll be there."

"And where is it?"

"You'll find it," the man said. "Just ask around."

"Okay," Trehearn said. He tossed back his brandy and stood up.

"That's no way to treat a good brandy," the other man said.

"Sorry," Trehearn said. "I'm a beer man."

"Have another and I'll show you how—"

"I have to go," Trehearn said. "I have to make sure the train is ready for Adams."

"You have until noon tomorrow," the man said. "Come on, Allan. Get two more brandies and I'll show you the proper way to drink it."

Trehearn looked down at the bald man, who was staring up at him expectantly.

"I tell you what," Trehearn said. "I'll get you another brandy, and me a beer. I'll watch you drink yours while I drink mine."

"Well, all right," the man said, "if that's as close as I'll get to my request, I'll take it."

"Wait right here," Trehearn said.

He walked to the bar, bought a beer and a brandy, but when he returned to the table, the bald man was gone.

FOUR

Clint walked to the bed, where Charlotte was kneeling. She was totally naked, heat emanating from her body. He took her full breasts into his hands, rubbed his thumbs over the nipples. She moaned and bit her bottom lip.

"You have too many clothes on," she said, putting her hands on his chest.

"Yeah, I do," he said. "You think you could help me with that?"

"Oh, I think so."

Her long, dark hair hung down past her shoulders in shimmering waves as she slipped off his jacket and began to unbutton his shirt. He had his little Colt New Line in his belt at the small of his back. He removed it and set it down on the night table next to the bed. Hanging on the bedpost was his gun and holster, which she had grown used to.

She peeled off his shirt, ran her hands over his bare chest, then leaned over and kissed him there. She licked his nipples, then kissed his belly, went to work on his belt.

When she had his trousers off and he was as naked as she was, she drew him down to the bed with her. From there they became lost in each other's bodies, as they had done each of the last two nights . . .

Trehearn reached the private railroad train the government had provided and climbed aboard. He tried the back door of the rearmost car and found it unlocked. He entered.

Two men jumped to their feet, both wearing uniforms of the United States Army. One was a corporal, and the other a sergeant.

"Sir!" the sergeant snapped.

"At ease, Sergeant," Trehearn said. "I'm not an officer, I'm just with State."

"Yessir!"

"Is this thing ready to go?"

"Yessir," the sergeant said.

"Where are the engineer and fireman?"

"Up front."

"And the conductor?"

"Somewhere . . . sir."

"Anyone else?"

"There's a cook, sir."

"And are you the only two soldiers?"

"Yessir."

"Are you assigned all the way to New York?"

"Yessir."

"Okay, good," Trehearn said. "Your man will be here at noon. His name's Clint Adams."

"The Gunsmith?" the corporal asked.

"That's right."

"At ease, Corporal," the sergeant said.

"Yessir."

"All right," Trehearn said. "Walk me through it, Sergeant."

"Yessir. This way, sir."

They walked through the car, transferred to the next. There was a dining car, a stock car, a coal car, and the engine.

Trehearn met the members of the crew, and approved of them. He then walked all the way back to the last car with the two soldiers.

"All right, men," he said. "You have the rest of the night to yourselves, as long as you're here at noon tomorrow. Got it?"

"We've got it, sir," the sergeant said.

Trehearn nodded to them and went out the door. All that was left now was to go back to his hotel, get a good night's sleep, and then catch a train the next morning.

Clint spread Charlotte's legs, then put her calves up on his shoulders. The hair between her legs was wispy, but as dark as the hair on her head. He used his fingers to part the hair and spread her pussy lips. Her sweet scent crept into his nose as he pressed his mouth to her. She was very wet, and he lapped it up while she writhed beneath him. She reached down to hold his head in place and gasped as he continued to work on her with his mouth, reveling in the taste of her.

When he felt the rippling of her muscles beneath him, and she began to buck and leap on the bed, he quickly mounted her and drove his hard cock into her heat. Her eyes went wide as waves of pleasure swept over her again and again. He slid his hands beneath her, cupped her buttocks, which were coated with her sweet wetness, and he proceeded to fuck her until they were both exhausted.

FIVE

In the morning, after she had awakened and crept into his arms, he told her that he had to leave.

"I thought you were going to be here another week," she asked.

"That was my original plan," he said, "but something's come up."

"What?"

"I've been called away," Clint said. "That's all I can say right now, Charlotte."

"I wish you had told me this last night," she said.

"Why? Would you have left?"

"No," she said, sliding her hand down between her legs and grasping him, "I would have kept you awake all night."

She stroked his cock until it was hard.

"Any chance you could take me with you?"

Mindful of the fact that she had him in her hand, he said, "I can't." And he didn't want to. He liked women, lots of women, but he never let himself become so attached to one that he'd take her with him.

"Well, in that case . . ."

She mounted him and slid down on him. She rode him hard, intending to give him something that would stay with him for a long, long time.

Clint went downstairs to the lobby and had himself some breakfast in the hotel dining room before checking out.

And since he didn't know when he'd be back, he decided to have a New Orleans breakfast. He still ordered his usual steak and eggs, but he also told the waiter to bring him an order of shrimp and grits.

He packed that breakfast away, then went upstairs to pack his things. Charlotte had returned to her own room, leaving behind her scent on the damp sheets. Too bad, he thought. Another few days with her would have been pleasant.

When he was packed, he checked out, had the doorman get him a horse-drawn cab. On the way to the train station, he told the driver to stop at a telegraph office.

"Wait for me," he said, leaving his bag in the carriage.

"Yessir."

Inside he wrote out his message and had the key operator send it to Washington D.C. Then he sent the same telegram to Labyrinth, Texas. For both he gave his return address as the Gotham Hotel, in New York.

"Okay," he told the driver, climbing back into the carriage, "the railway station."

"Yessir."

* * *

At the station, he picked up the ticket that was waiting for him at the ticket booth. The government train did not provide him with a sleeping compartment or a berth, so he was going to have to sit up all the way to New York.

He got aboard, satisfied to find that no one would be traveling in the car with him. If it stayed that way, he'd be able to stretch out to sleep later.

He still couldn't place the name "Ellen Terry," but the name "Henry Irving" was starting to become familiar. He'd been to theaters in New York, Washington, Denver, San Francisco, and other places. Maybe he had seen the name in one of them—or more than one. If Irving was such a famous actor in England, he'd be known in theater circles here. Clint suddenly thought of another telegram he could have sent. Maybe he'd have time to do that when the train stopped in Saint Louis.

The train jerked, and then started. He was on his way.

As he'd hoped, he had about a half-hour stop when he reached Saint Louis. He found a telegraph office near the railroad station and sent a third telegram to San Francisco. The recipient there was an actress he knew who was fairly successful, mostly for her beauty, not her talent. He asked her about Henry Irving and Ellen Terry, then asked her to respond to him at the Gotham Hotel.

He got something to eat in the train station, then reboarded his train. This time there were two other passengers in his car, military men in uniforms. He hoped they wouldn't be talkative.

He pulled his hat down over his eyes to try to dissuade them.

By the time the train pulled into New York, his fellow passengers had decided he was antisocial. They had not once tried to engage him in conversation. Clint waited for them to disembark, then rose to his feet, feeling grimy and in need of a bath.

He had arrived two days ahead of Henry Irving and Ellen Terry.

SIX

"I thought we were to be met at the dock," Ellen Terry said.

"We will be," Henry Irving said.

They stood on the dock with their bags around their feet. People were stopping to look at the well-dressed couple: a handsome man in his forties, and a very beautiful woman in her thirties, her hair tucked up under a hat so that her fine, long neck was there for all to see.

"Then where is he?" she asked. "Or she? Or them?"

"This is America, Ellen," Irving said. "No one is on time. Just be patient, my dear."

New York had gotten bigger, more crowded, and it had taken Clint longer than he'd expected to get to the docks. When he reached the boat, he saw people waiting on the dock, but immediately knew who his two were. They were standing still, their heads held high, eyes raking the crowd. The man was as calm as he seemed. The woman, though, was agitated.

Clint walked over to them. She saw him coming and lifted her chin even higher. She said something to the man, and he turned his head. He had a noble profile.

"Mr. Irving?" Clint asked. "Miss Terry?"

"Yes, I am Henry Irving," the man said. "This is Miss Ellen Terry."

Clint nodded to the both of them, then touched his fingers to his hat, but the woman wasn't looking.

"My name is Clint Adams," he said. "I'll be your . . . escort while you're in our country."

"Escort?" Ellen Terry asked. "I thought you were to be our bodyguard."

"Well, that, too," Clint said. He looked down at the collection of bags that surrounded them. "Are all these bags yours?"

"Of course they are!" Terry snapped.

"Actually," Irving said, "most of them belong to the lovely lady."

"I get some teamsters to help carry them to the carriage," Clint said.

"Why did you not come here with them?" Terry asked.

"I didn't know how many you had," Clint said. "I thought I might be able to handle them myself."

Irving laughed and said, "Obviously, you have never traveled with an actress."

"Actually," Clint said, "I have, but American actresses."

"Yes, well," Irving said, "I imagine they are quite different."

"Just wait here," Clint said. "I'll be right back."

"You are going to leave us unattended?" Ellen Terry asked.

"Just for a few minutes," Clint said with a smile. "Try to stay out of trouble."

He turned and walked away.

"Such insolence!" Ellen Terry said.

"He can afford to be insolent," Irving said. "Do you know who that is, my dear?"

"I didn't pay attention to his name," she said.

"You should have," Irving said. "His name is Clint Adams."

"Should that mean something to me?" she asked.

"It would if you knew anything about the West," Irving said. "He is called the Gunsmith."

"A gunsmith?" she repeated. "They sent someone who fixes guns to accompany us?"

"Not a gunsmith, my dear," Irving said. "The Gunsmith. He is a legend in the West for his prowess with a pistol—and, I believe, with women."

"Hmph," she said, "a ruffian like him?"

"Actually," Irving said, "he seemed quite smooth to me."

"Then you are easily impressed."

"We will see."

Clint found three men to help with the luggage, gave them a dollar each, and brought them back to where Irving and Terry were still waiting. Ellen Terry still had her nose high in the air.

"This way, folks," Clint said. "They're bringing the bags."

"Be careful with that trunk!" Ellen Terry snapped at them.

"Yes, ma'am."

"Aren't you going to supervise them?" she asked Clint.

"They know what they're doing, ma'am," he said. "I want to get you to the carriage as quickly as possible."

He started walking, hoping that they were following.

This job was not going to be a walk in the park.

SEVEN

Clint got Irving and Terry situated in the carriage, and then supervised the men as they piled the bags up on top. Terry stuck her head out the window and kept up a running criticism of their work.

"My dear," Irving said at one point, "bring your head back inside and relax."

"I don't want them to leave any of my bags behind," she said impatiently, "or damage any of them."

"This is what they do," Irving said. "Everything will be fine. Besides, this time Mr. Adams is supervising them, as you wanted."

"I hardly think he's qualified," she complained.

Irving shook his head as she stuck her head back out the window and started snapping at everyone again.

"You gonna be working for her for long?" one of the men asked Clint.

"Oh, yeah," Clint said. "She's my cross to bear."

"Take my advice," the man said, "and put her over your knee the first chance you get. That's what a woman like that needs."

"I just might follow that little piece of advice," Clint said.

He gave each of the men another dollar, then got into the carriage with Irving and Terry.

"You propose to ride inside, with us?" Ellen Terry asked in surprise.

"Ma'am," Clint said, "we're going to be riding all over this country together, and I expect to share all the same accommodations with you. If that's all right with you?"

"It most certainly isn't," she said with a sniff, "but I suppose I have little to say about it."

Irving gave Clint a pitying look. Clint felt sorry for the actor, having to come all this way on a boat with her.

He banged on the wall of the carriage for the driver to start up.

Clint took them to the same hotel he was staying at, the Gotham. Clint had a very official-looking letter that told the hotel they were to bill the United States government for all expenses. Of course, Trehearn—as well as Ellen Terry—had expected Clint to take them to the best hotel in the city, but Clint decided against it.

He walked them to their rooms, first Ellen Terry, then Henry Irving.

As they entered Ellen Terry's room, she stopped short and looked around with a disgusted expression on her face.

"These are my accommodations?" she asked.

"For now."

"This was the best you could do?"

"No, ma'am, it wasn't," Clint said. "But this is where I wanted to put you."

"You wanted to put us?" Terry asked. "Since when do you make those decisions?"

"Since I became responsible for your welfare."

"You are also," she said, "responsible for my comfort!"

"I'll see that extra pillows are sent up," he said. "Good night."

He pulled the door shut, joining Irving in the hall. They both heard something shatter against the door.

"I am sorry, old chap," Irving said, "but she is a bit temperamental."

"That's a bit?" Clint asked.

"She is a wonderful actress, though," Irving went on, "and quite a charming woman when you come to know her better."

"Mr. Irving, no offense," Clint said, "but I don't think that woman and I are going to come to know each other better."

He took the actor to his room, down the hall. Clint had a room between the two actors.

"This will do," Irving said as they entered. It was the same room Terry had.

"I didn't want to put you in the best hotel in town because that's what people expect."

"What people would that be, dear boy?"

"Well," Clint said, "anybody who wants to do you harm."

"My good fellow," Irving said, "I seriously doubt that anyone would want to do either of us harm. I believe our two governments are just being overly cautious."

"Well, there's nothing wrong with that," Clint said. "Precautions are important."

"Yes, well," Irving said, removing his jacket and his purple cravat, "I suspect a man in your position would feel that way."

"My position?"

"I know who you are, you see," Irving said. "I'm quite pleased that your government chose a legend of the Old West to safeguard us. I don't feel it was necessary, but I look forward to many evenings of chatting with you about your adventures."

"My adventures?"

"But of course," Irving said. "Your feats of derring-do, as it were. I say, have you ever thought about stepping on the stage?"

"My friend Bill Cody has been trying to get me to do that for years."

"Buffalo Bill Cody?" Irving said, almost with glee.

"That's the one."

"Oh, my good man," Irving said with delight, "we are going to have many hours of conversation, aren't we?"

"I'll check back with you a little later on, sir. I'll go and make sure all your luggage is brought up.

Clint stepped out into the hall. He didn't know what was going to be worse—Ellen Terry not feeling he was worth talking to at all, or Henry Irving wanting to hear about his feats of derring-do.

EIGHT

Clint made sure all of Ellen Terry's bags were delivered to her room. He remained outside, where he could hear her berating the poor bellmen who had brought them up.

They moved on to Irving's room next. He knocked and the tall actor opened the door.

"Ah, my bags," he said. "How delightful."

The bellmen brought in his two bags, and one trunk, and Clint noticed that he tipped them nicely.

"Clint, I wonder if you would stay a minute."

"Of course."

He walked the bellmen to the door, then closed it firmly behind them.

"I wonder if we might repair downstairs to the bar for a drink."

"You want a drink?" Clint asked. "I can have something brought up—"

"No, no, you don't understand," Irving said, "I want to drink among . . . the people."

"You mean . . . the common people?"

Irving had the good braces to look abashed.

"Yes, I suppose I do sound like a right snob, don't I?" he asked. "Let me explain. I am an actor, and the way I learn my craft is to watch people as they move about every day. Ordinary people."

"I understand."

"I probably still sound a right pratt, but I would like to go downstairs for a drink."

"All right," Clint said. "Just let me go to my room first to freshen up."

"I tell you what," Irving said, "why don't we wait until after dark?"

"Suits me," Clint said. He figured they could have a drink, and then get something to eat. "I'll come back in a couple of hours."

"Excellent," Irving said. "I have to have a change of clothes myself."

"All right," Clint said. "And I better check on her ladyship, as well, before we leave."

"Good luck."

"I'll need it."

He left Irving's room and walked to his own. He entered, put his back against his door, and took a deep breath. He wasn't ready to deal with Ellen Terry again, not at that moment.

Later, he walked to Ellen Terry's room and knocked.

"Come."

He opened the door and entered. She was seated in

front of a low table with a mirror. Her hair was down past her shoulders, and she was brushing it. She was wearing some sort of dressing gown. Beneath it her body appeared soft and supple. The room's windows were dark, as the sun had gone down.

She regarded him in the mirror.

"What do you want?" she asked.

"I was going to ask you the same thing," he said. "Henry and I are going down for a drink. Would you like to come?"

"To a common bar?" she asked, arching her eyebrows. "No, thank you."

"Suit yourself."

She turned quickly on her stool and said, "I am hungry, however. If you could have some food sent up. Lobster, perhaps?"

"I'll see what I can do. Something will be up shortly."

She nodded and turned back to the mirror without a thank-you.

Clint went to his own room, determined to have steak sent up to her.

He changed his clothes and then walked to Irving's door. He knocked, but when it was opened, it was not the actor, but a bearded man who looked as if he had just come off the docks.

"What the hell—" Clint started.

"Don't get excited, Clint," the man said in Henry Irving's voice. "It is me."

Clint narrowed his eyes and stared at the man. Eventually, he saw past the facial hair to the man behind the makeup.

"That's amazing," he said.

"It is what I do," Irving said. "Come in, please."

Clint entered and closed the door. In the center of the room Irving's trunk lay open. Inside were what seemed like dozens of wigs, all types of facial hair—mustaches, muttonchops, eyebrows—and what looked to be all kinds of skin blemishes, from rash to pimple to mole.

"Just let me put on my hat and we can go," Irving said. "I'm anxious to have a beer with you."

"Beer?" Clint asked. "Not brandy?"

"No, sir," the man said to Clint in an entirely different voice. Gone was the aristocratic Henry Irving, and in his place an American of indeterminate age and class. "I feel like havin' me a cold beer." Then he adjusted his stovepipe hat and added, "Let's get goin', partner."

Clint shook his head, opened the door for Irving, and then followed him down the hall.

NINE

Downstairs in the lobby, Clint told Irving to wait while he ordered Ellen Terry some food.

"I told her I'd have it brought up to her room," he added.

"That was kind of you," Irving said. "Did she ask for lobster?"

"Yes."

"She always asks for lobster."

"Well, she's getting steak."

Irving just laughed.

Clint walked over to the dining room and talked to the maître d'.

"Yes, sir, of course," the man told him. "I will see to it immediately."

"Thanks." He walked back to Irving, who was drawing stares in the lobby. He was wearing a wig that made his hair look like it was shoulder-length, and had affixed a huge mole to his cheek.

"Let's get that beer."

Irving followed Clint into the bar.

The Gotham may not have been one of New York's top luxury hotels, but it did a lot of out-of-town business. The bar was about three-quarters filled with traveling businessmen. As Clint and Irving entered, they drew looks because Irving's outfit was replete with a cape.

They walked to the bar and Clint ordered two beers. He handed one to Irving.

"What name goes with this look?" Clint asked. "Or should I just call you Henry?"

"What would be a good American name?" Irving replied.

"Jack," Clint said.

"Why would you choose that name?"

Clint shrugged.

"It just came to me."

"Yes, well," Irving said, "I think I'll modify it. Call me . . . Jacko."

"Jacko is not an American name," Clint pointed out.

"It doesn't matter," Irving said. "This was just a lark for tonight. This character will go back into my trunk when I return to my room." Irving looked around. "Are these the usual types of people one finds in an American saloon?"

"You're probably interested in Western saloons, Henry," Clint said. "You'll see enough of them, I'm sure. What does your schedule look like?"

"Not sure, really," Irving said. "I know we're performing here, Philadelphia, Washington, Boston—not in that order, of course. And then we'll begin to work our way west."

"Boston?" Clint asked. "I'd think that would be your first stop, and then work your way south to Philadelphia and Washington."

"Yes, that sounds like it," Irving said. "I will check the itinerary in my room."

They finished their beer as the conversations around them seemed to become louder and louder.

"I think I am ready to return to my room," Irving said. "I'm quite hungry."

"So am I," Clint said. "Would you like to eat in the dining room, or up in your room?"

"This makeup is very effective on stage," Irving said, "but it is not conducive to eating. I believe I will dine in my room, as Ellen is."

"All right," Clint said. "I'll eat in the dining room, and have something sent up. Lobster?"

"No," Irving said with a laugh, "a steak is just fine."

TEN

Clint repeated the process with the maître d', ordered a steak dinner to be delivered to Henry Irving's room, and then asked the man to seat him. It was supper time but he was able to choose his own table. He grabbed one in the back, and could survey the entire room from there.

He ordered coffee while he waited for his steak, and studied the other people in the room. Most of them were probably guests at the hotel. The Gotham did not get a lot of local business.

In addition to the entire room, Clint was able to see part of the lobby from his table, and the front door. He was almost finished with his steak when he thought he saw Henry Irving walk by, heading out. He hurriedly paid his bill, and rushed out to catch sight of him.

Irving was walking down the street briskly. Clint had seen his profile, knew he was not in makeup, but he was wearing a cape and top hat, and carrying a walking stick.

Clint decided not to try to catch up with the man, but rather to follow him and see what he was up to.

The Gotham was a full ten blocks from the theater district, and Clint expected Irving to walk that way, but instead he walked over to Tenth Avenue first, and then uptown. They reached an area where girls were working the street, and as Clint watched, Irving stopped and spoke with several of them.

Suddenly, as Clint watched, Irving and a girl stepped into an alley. Clint rushed to the mouth of the alley and looked in, but it was totally dark. He hesitated, waiting for his eyes to adjust to the dark, then entered the alley. He reached the end—a blank wall—without finding Irving or the girl.

He made his way back, stopping at several doors and windows he passed, but they were all locked up tight.

He came back out to Tenth Avenue, unsure about what to do next. Irving's welfare was his job, and he had allowed the man to disappear.

He decided all that was left for him to do was go back to the hotel and wait to see when Henry Irving returned from his nocturnal walk.

He began to retrace his steps to the Gotham.

He went into the bar when he got there, ordered a beer, and then got himself a table from where he could watch the lobby. Irving had to come back in the front door, and Clint wouldn't miss him.

It took a couple of hours, but Irving finally returned.

He walked briskly in the front door and Clint moved quickly. Once again, however, he decided not to stop the man. Why let him know he had seen him? He was interested in what would happen the next morning when he asked Irving how he spent his night. Would he admit to taking a walk?

Clint watched the man walk to the Gotham's elevator. As the doors closed, Clint went to the stairs and took them two at a time. He arrived on the third floor before the elevator opened. He watched from cover while Irving walked down the hall, past Ellen Terry's room, past Clint's door, and then let himself into his own room.

Hoping that the man was in for the night—he couldn't very well sit in the lobby all night and keep watch—Clint unlocked his own door and went inside. Just for a moment he wondered if Ellen Terry was in her room, and then decided he needed to check.

He left his room, walked to her door, and wondered if he would be waking her. He pressed his ear to the door, didn't hear anything. Would a grown woman—an actress from Europe—be asleep at this time? Maybe, if she was tired out from the trip across the ocean.

In the end he decided not to knock, and just assumed she was in there, asleep.

He went back to his own door, stopped, and for a moment wondered if he should knock on Irving's. He was sure to be awake after his walk.

He decided to do it, under the pretense of finding out if Irving had gotten his food. He walked to the actor's door and knocked. Irving answered immediately.

"Mr. Adams! May I call you Clint?" he was free of

any theatrical makeup, and was wearing a dressing gown that looked like silk. "What can I do for you?"

"I just wanted to make sure you got your meal."

"I did," Irving said. "It was a very good steak, and the bellman has already picked up the tray. Thank you."

"How have you been spending your evening?"

"I'm reading," Irving said. "Going over some of the pieces that Ellen and I will be doing in our show."

"Do you memorize all that stuff?"

"Oh, yes," Irving said. "I'm just refreshing my memory."

"I see," Clint said. "Well, I'll stop by in the morning. We can go to breakfast and discuss your itinerary."

"Excellent," Irving said. "We will see you then."

Clint took a quick look around the room. No sign of the cape, top hat, or walking stick he had seen Irving with earlier.

"Is that all, Clint?"

"Yes," Clint said, "that's all, Henry. Good night."

Clint went back to his room. His first day with his charges had been very interesting. He wondered what the rest of the time would be like.

ELEVEN

In the morning, Clint rose earlier, washed and dressed, then went down the hall to Irving's room. He knocked, then knocked again. No answer.

"Henry!"

No answer.

"Mr. Irving!" he pounded on the door. He was about to kick it in when suddenly it opened. Clint half expected to see a woman in the room, maybe even Ellen Terry, but it was just Henry Irving.

"I'm sorry," the man said. "I don't sleep well, but when I do, I sleep deeply."

"Then I'm sorry I woke you."

"Nonsense," Irving said. "Why don't you go and rouse Ellen, and by the time you get back, I'll be dressed."

"All right," Clint said. "I hope she's easier to rouse than you were."

"Don't worry," Irving said. "Ellen is a light sleeper."

"Okay, see you in a while."

Irving nodded and closed the door. Clint walked past his door to Ellen Terry's and knocked.

"Come!" she said.

Clint opened the door slowly and stuck his head in.

"Are you decent?" he asked.

"I am," she said, "and that apparently makes one of us."

He entered and closed the door. Ellen Terry must have been up for a while. She was dressed, wearing a long, high-necked dress, her hair piled high atop her head once again.

"I came to take you to breakfast," he said.

"Just you and me?" she asked. "How presumptuous."

"No," he said, "the three of us. Henry's getting dressed."

"I see."

"We'll discuss your itinerary."

"Yes, I suppose we should," she said. "Very well." She grabbed her purse. "Ready?"

"Henry needs time to dress," he said.

"No," she said, "he doesn't. That's one thing about the theater, Mr. Adams. It teaches you to get dressed very quickly."

"Well, okay," I said. "You know him better than I do." He opened the door for her, and she swept past him without a word.

"You're welcome," he said.

As Terry had predicted, Irving was fully dressed—and looking impeccable—when he opened his door again. Still no hat and stick, though.

They went downstairs to the dining room and were seated immediately. It was early, and only several other tables were occupied.

A waiter came by and gave them their menus.

"Coffee, Miss Terry?" Clint asked.

"Tea, Mr. Adams," she said as if he had asked a stupid question.

"Of course," Clint said. "Tea for the lady. Henry?"

"Also tea," Irving told the waiter.

"And I'll have coffee."

"What would an American breakfast be?" Irving asked.

The waiter looked at Clint, to see if he would be answering that question.

"Bacon and eggs," Clint said, "ham and eggs, flapjacks—"

"And which do you eat?" the actor asked.

"I usually order steak and eggs."

"Then that's what I shall have," Irving said, handing the waiter the menu. "Steak and eggs, please."

Once she had determined there was no blood sausage or bangers available, Ellen Terry ordered one egg and one slice of ham.

"Yes, ma'am. How would you like the egg?"

"Poached, of course."

She got her poached egg because they were in New York. Clint wondered how she'd react when they got farther west and eggs were available only one of two ways, and both prepared in a frying pan.

The waiter went off to place their orders, then returned with a basket of warm biscuits, butter, and marmalade.

"Ah," Terry said, reaching for the preserves. "Something civilized."

Clint watched her slice a biscuit in half, cover both halves with marmalade, and then eat them with gusto. With that kind of appetite, he wondered why she had ordered only one egg and one slice of ham.

TWELVE

"You were correct, Clint," Irving said.

"About what?" He looked away from Terry, who was doctoring another biscuit, and looked at Irving.

"Our itinerary." Irving took a folded sheaf of papers from inside his jacket. "Boston is first, then we are to go south to Philadelphia, and Washington D.C."

"And then west?"

"That's right," Irving said. "Saint Louis, Kansas City, Dallas . . . some other cities I don't recognize . . . and then we finish in Tombstone."

"Tombstone?"

"Yes," Irving said, still reading, "at a place called the Birdcage." Irving looked at him. "Do you know it?"

"Very well," Clint said, "but it's not what it used to be."

"I wanted to play some historic locations in the West," Irving said.

"Well, I don't know who prepared your schedule, but

you got your wish with the Birdcage. Lillian Russell and Lily Langtry both played there. And Doc Holliday dealt faro there."

"Sounds quite exciting," Irving said.

"Sounds dusty," Ellen Terry said.

"My dear," Irving said, "why ever did you agree to this tour?"

She smiled across the table at him and said, "Why, to be with you, of course, my dear." She popped a piece of biscuit into her mouth.

"I'd like a copy of that schedule," Clint said.

"I will make you one," Irving promised, and tucked the sheets of paper back into his jacket.

The waiter came with their respective breakfasts, and they ate.

When they were finished, Clint asked, "When and where are you performing first?"

"The Lyceum, on Fourth Avenue," Irving said.

"Why that one?"

"It's completely lit by electricity," Irving said. "The only such theater in the U.S."

"Well," Clint said, "that sounds like the place to perform first."

"Also, it is the name of my theater in London," Irving said. "It seems fitting."

"When shall we be looking at the theater, Henry?" Terry asked.

"Well, if it's all right with Mr. Adams," Irving said, "I'd like to go over there right away. Our performance is to be at eight p.m. tonight."

"Hey, that's fine with me," Clint said.

Ellen Terry looked at him and asked, "Will you be dressing like that?"

Clint looked back at her, then said, "I think I can find a jacket."

"Will you have your gun on?" Henry Irving asked.

"This is New York, Henry, not the West," Clint said. "I'll have a gun on me, but not my holster."

"Perhaps we will get to see this vaunted ability of yours with a gun?" Terry asked.

"Miss Terry," Clint said, "I sincerely hope not."

They left the hotel and had the doorman get them a cab. Clint held the door open for Ellen Terry and assisted her in with a hand on her elbow. Henry Irving climbed in next, and then Clint.

"The Lyceum Theater," Clint told the driver. "Fourth Avenue."

"Yessir."

They rode in silence while Ellen Terry looked out the window at the passing streets, and the people. She had a look of disdain on her face the entire way. Apparently, New York was not living up to her standards.

"Have you been here before?" Clint asked Henry Irving.

"No," Irving said, "this is our first time. I hope that the people of your country like what we have to offer."

Clint looked at Ellen Terry's profile, which was beautiful.

"I think the men will like what she has to offer," Clint said. "You might have to win them over with your talent, though."

Irving laughed. "That is usually the case. My beast to Ellen's beauty."

"I didn't mean—"

"I know what you meant," Irving said. "I was handsome once, in my youth. These days I must rely heavily on my talent. Luckily, that has not waned."

Neither had the man's ego, Clint noticed.

THIRTEEN

Clint sat in the empty Lyceum Theater and watched as Henry Irving put everyone through their paces—the theater owners, the director, the lighting people, the set design people . . . and Ellen Terry.

He found it all very interesting, Irving telling everyone where to stand, what to do, and—in Ellen Terry's case—what to say.

Suddenly, Terry started to shout.

"I know what to say, Henry!" she snapped. "I always know what to say."

"Calm down, dear girl—"

"No," she said, "you can tell all these people what to do, but you can't tell me. I know what to do." She dropped the papers she was holding. "I'll leave you to work with them. I'll be back when it's time to go on."

With that, she stormed off the stage.

Clint was confused. Was she leaving the stage, or the

building? Should he stay with Henry or go with her? He got up from his seat and walked up to the stage.

"Henry, is she leaving?"

"I'm afraid so," Irving said. "Clint, why don't you make sure she gets back to the hotel all right. I still have a few hours of work here. You can come back and get me later."

"Okay, Henry," Clint said.

He climbed up onto the stage, then ran off in the same direction Ellen Terry had gone.

Backstage he looked around for her, afraid she may have already left the building. Then suddenly, he caught sight of her.

"Ellen!"

She turned to see who had called out her name. She'd obviously gone back to her dressing room, as she was dressed for the street.

"What is it?"

He walked up to her.

"You can't leave by yourself."

"I'm a big girl, Mr. Adams," she assured him. "I will be fine."

"That may be so, but I can't let you go out in the streets of New York alone. If you want to go back to the hotel, I'll take you."

She frowned at him, looked as if she was about to argue, then changed her mind.

"Oh, all right," she said. "Come along."

She headed for the stage door, and he followed.

Outside she hurried up the alley toward Fourth Avenue He ran after her and grabbed her arm, virtually yanking her to a stop.

"Whoa!" he said.

"Let me go!"

"Where do you think you're going?"

"I want to walk before I go back to the hotel to change for the performance."

"Walk where?"

"Just walk down the streets," she said. "Can we do that?"

"Well . . . sure," he said. "Why not? But you can't just walk anywhere. We can walk in the direction of the hotel, and eventually get a cab."

"Very well. Then show me which way to go," she demanded.

"This way . . ." Clint said.

When the man across the street saw Ellen Terry come out of the alley, he was elated. However, it faded the very next second when Clint Adams came out behind her.

The woman looked like she wanted to run, but Adams grabbed her arm. When they finally decided to walk, the man made up his mind to wait and see if Henry Irving would come out alone.

He decided to let Terry and Clint Adams go—for now.

Clint walked with Ellen Terry on Fourth Avenue for a while, then took her to Fifth Avenue. The architecture was different from London, which he had visited before. But if he was looking for her to be impressed, it didn't happen. She did not seem the least bit interested in what she was seeing, and that made him wonder why she had wanted to walk at all.

Abruptly, she turned to him and said, "I need to go back to the hotel and get ready for the performance."

"All right," Clint said.

He flagged down a passing cab and they rode to the hotel in silence.

FOURTEEN

When they got to the hotel, Clint walked Terry to her door.

"I will need about two hours," she said. "I assume you'll be wanting to escort me back?"

"I will."

"Well then, you had better go get Henry and bring him back so he can get cleaned up," she suggested, "then you can escort both of us back."

Before he could say a word, she slammed the door in his face. He didn't know if Terry disliked Americans, men, or just him.

He went downstairs and had a beer before going back to the theater to get Irving. As the bartender handed him a beer, he said, "That fellow's been waiting for you to get back."

"What fella?" Clint asked.

"That one walking over here."

Clint turned his head to look. A man had just gotten

up from a table and was walking toward him, carrying a beer of his own. He was wearing a black suit and a bowler hat.

"Mr. Adams?" he asked. He was tall, not yet forty, moved with the ease of a man who could take care of himself.

"That's right."

"My name is Inspector Gibbons. I'm with the New York City Police."

Clint looked at the beer in the man's left hand.

"You got a badge that proves that?"

Gibbons moved the beer to his right hand, moved his jacket aside with his left so Clint could see the badge pinned to his shirt.

"You always wear it on your shirt?" Clint asked.

"I thought you might ask for it," Gibbons said, allowing his jacket to fall closed.

"Well, Inspector," Clint said, "why don't I buy you a fresh cold beer to replace that flat one and then you can tell me what I can do for you."

"That sounds good," the inspector said. He put the flat beer on the bar and the bartender gave him a cold one. "Thank you."

"Can we talk right here at the bar?" Clint asked. Not that the place was crowded; it wasn't. Clint just wanted to get this over with as soon as possible.

"Sure, why not?" Gibbons asked. "I received a telegram from a policeman I know in London. He told me they were sending two of their national treasures over here to perform. That's what he said. National treasures. Do you know who that might be?"

"I do," Clint said, "but how did you know?"

"Well, when I got that telegram, I sent off one of my own, to Washington. I figured if someone like that was coming to New York, I should know about it."

"And what did they tell you?"

"Same thing," Gibbons said. "National treasures. But they also told me you'd be here watching out for them."

"And they told you what hotel I was in?"

"No, I found that out by myself."

"Well," Clint said, "I guess you are a detective."

"That I am," Gibbons said. "Now, do you mind telling me what these national treasures are?"

"I don't see why not," Clint said, "since you are the police."

"I was hoping you'd feel that way."

"They're people."

"I beg your pardon?"

"Actors," Clint said. "Henry Irving and Ellen Terry. Apparently they're very famous."

Gibbons frowned. "I never heard of them."

"Well, they'll be performing at the Lyceum Theater tonight," Clint said. "You can see for yourself, firsthand, why the British consider them to be national treasures."

"So, why would you concern yourself with them?"

"I was asked by the Department of State to make sure nothing happens to them while they're here," Clint said.

"In New York?"

"In the country," Clint said. "They'll be touring here for quite a while."

"And you'll be with them the whole time?"

"Every step of the way," Clint said.

Gibbons sipped his beer while he gave the situation some thought.

"I'm sure I could arrange to have a ticket for you at the box office," Clint said. "Just say the word."

"I'm not much for the theater," Gibbons said. "I'll take your word for it that they're actors."

"Well, I'll try to make sure there's no trouble while they're in New York."

"I'd appreciate that." Apparently, the inspector wasn't much for beer either. He set this one down on the bar, virtually untouched. "Thanks for your time, Mr. Adams."

"No problem," Clint said. "Always willing to assist the police."

Gibbons nodded, and strode out of the bar without further word. Clint thought the incident was odd, but set it aside and headed for the theater to pick up Irving.

FIFTEEN

When Clint arrived at the theater and entered, Henry Irving was right where he'd left him, on stage. Clint stood in the back of the theater and watched as Irving continued giving instructions for the night's performance. When he couldn't wait any longer, Clint walked to the front.

"Ah, Clint," Irving said, spotting him. "I was hoping you would come back for me. Where is Ellen?"

"She's at the hotel, getting herself ready."

"Well then, that is where I should be," Irving said. He came down off the stage and took Clint by the arm. "Come along, then."

They walked outside together, and Clint flagged down a cab. They were easy to find in that district because of the theaters.

As they rode back, Irving asked, "How was Ellen?"

"How is she always around me?" Clint asked. "Ornery."

"That's because she likes you."

Clint laughed.

"That's how she treats men she likes?"

"How much do you know about women?"

"A lot, actually."

"Well," Irving said, "how much do you know about Englishwomen?"

"Not that much," Clint admitted.

"Take it from me," Irving said. "She likes you."

"If that's how she treats a man she likes," Clint said, "let's hope she doesn't fall in love with me. It might be the death of me."

As the cab approached the hotel, Clint told Irving about his conversation with Inspector Gibbons.

"A policeman?"

"Yes. Apparently he got a telegram from one of your policemen. I suppose they want him to look out for you."

"But I have you to do that," Irving said. "And I am quite satisfied with that."

"Thanks."

The cab stopped in front of the hotel and they got out. As it started to pull away, there was a shot. Clint heard it and moved immediately, tackling Irving and taking him to the ground.

"What the blazes—"

"Lie still!" Clint commanded him.

He looked at the buildings across the street, the doorways and windows, and the rooftops, for a shooter. There was no one in sight. Apparently whoever it was had taken the one shot and run.

"What the hell was that? A shot?" Irving asked from the ground.

"Yes, it was."

Clint stood up then helped the actor to his feet.

"Was it meant for you, or me?" Irving asked.

"I don't know."

"Well," Irving said, "luckily he missed."

"Actually," Clint said, pointing, "he didn't. Not completely."

He pointed to where the cab driver was lying. The bullet had taken him from his seat and tossed him to the ground. Clint could see that he was dead.

"Poor fellow."

"He must have pulled away just as the shot was fired," Clint said. "He got in the way."

"Saving one of us," Irving said.

Yes, Clint thought, but which one?

"I think it's time to send for Inspector Gibbons," Clint said.

SIXTEEN

Clint had the doorman send someone for the police.

"Shall I wait?" Irving said.

"No," Clint said. "Go to your room and get yourself ready. If Gibbons wants to talk to you, he can come up there."

"Very well."

Clint didn't want Irving out where another shot could be attempted.

He waited in the lobby for the police to arrive. Gibbons walked in the front door with two uniformed men.

"What happened?" he asked. "The bellman said something about a shot."

"Henry Irving and I were getting out of a cab when someone took a shot at us. He missed, but hit the driver."

"Which one of you was the target?"

"I don't know," Clint said. "I suppose there's a good chance it was me."

"Because of your reputation, you mean."

"Yes."

"But it could have been the actor," Gibbons said. "The national treasure."

"I suppose so."

"I've got men across the street, trying to find something," Gibbons said. "And we're removing the body."

"The driver was hit by accident. He got between us and the shooter."

"Who knows?" Gibbons asked. "Maybe he was the target. Maybe he owes somebody money, or was sleeping with somebody's wife."

"Well," Clint said, "I guess that's your job to find out."

"I'll find out," Gibbons said. "When we talked earlier, I didn't ask you how long you would be in New York with your actors."

"I'm pretty sure they only have this one performance tonight. I suppose we'll leave tomorrow or the next day."

"For where?"

"Boston next."

"And then?"

"Philadelphia and Washington. After that, we'll be heading west."

"I'd like to talk to Mr. Irving before I go," Gibbons said.

"He's in his room, getting ready," Clint said. "Come on."

When Irving opened the door, he smiled and said to Clint, "This must be our friend the inspector."

"Gibbons," the man said. "Inspector Gibbons. I'm pleased to meet you, Mr. Irving."

"Come on in," Irving said to them both. "I'm almost ready."

They entered and Clint closed the door. Irving was wearing a black suit and a white shirt.

"What costume is this?" Clint asked.

"No costume, I'm afraid," he said. "Ellen and I are doing readings from several different plays, so we won't be in costume for any particular characters."

"I see."

"Mr. Adams has told me what he saw downstairs after the shot was fired," Gibbons said. "I'd like to know what you saw."

"I saw the sidewalk," Irving said. "Clint pushed me down and shielded me with his body. Luckily, there was not a second shot."

"So you didn't see anyone?"

"I'm afraid not," Irving said. "Not before or after the shot. Oh, except for the poor driver. Do you know his name?"

"Not yet."

"When you do, I'd like to send flowers to the family."

"I'll let you know where you can send them."

"Thank you."

"Anything else?" Clint asked.

"No," Gibbons said, "that's it."

"I'll walk you back down," Clint said.

"I'll get Ellen and meet you in the lobby, Clint," Irving said.

"No," Clint said, "just wait up here in your rooms until I come to get you."

"All right."

Gibbons had already stepped into the hall when Clint said, “In fact, maybe I can convince you to cancel your performance tonight.”

“Oh, no,” Irving said. “We did not come all this way to be frightened off by one shot. The show must go on, Clint.”

“I was afraid you'd say that.”

SEVENTEEN

Clint walked Gibbons all the way out to the street. The body had been removed. There was blood on the sidewalk.

"The hotel should have someone clean that off," Gibbons said.

"I'm sure they will."

"Mr. Adams," the inspector said, "try not to get shot at again while you're in New York. I would appreciate it."

"So would I, Inspector." Clint said. "So would I."

Clint went back upstairs, found Henry Irving and Ellen Terry in her room, waiting for him.

"You're supposed to be protecting us!" she snarled at him.

"I'm sorry, ma'am, but—"

"How could you let Henry be shot at?"

"You're not being very fair, my dear," Irving said.

"How was he to know someone would take a shot at me?"

"It's his job to know."

"Besides," Irving went on, "they could have been shooting at him."

"I don't care—"

"I think we should get going," Clint said. "You can continue to berate me on the way, but it might distract me and that wouldn't be good. You know, just in case someone takes a shot at you this time."

She closed her mouth and glared at him.

"Let's go, love," Irving said, taking her arm.

Clint declined a front row seat, chose instead to watch from backstage, where he could also watch the audience. He didn't pay much attention to Irving and Terry's performances, but enough to be impressed by their delivery. Also, by their ability to remember all the scenes from different plays.

Most of his attention was on the audience, just in case there was a shooter there. However, by the end of the night, it was obvious by the standing ovation they received that everyone in the audience enjoyed them.

Terry came off the stage first and said bitterly, "I kept waiting for someone to shoot me!"

"It didn't show," Clint said. "You were very good."

She glared at him and demanded, "How would you know?"

"You also look very beautiful tonight."

That stopped her. She stared at him silently for a few moments, then turned and stalked off toward her dressing room.

Henry Irving took extra bows—he was, after all, the star—and then came off, smiling at Clint.

"How did it go for you?" Irving asked.

"Fine," Clint said. "My part was a success. Nobody shot at you. How about your part?"

"It went very well," he said.

There was an odd shuffling noise in the air, and Clint realized it was the sound of the crowd filing out.

"We will be ready to go back to the hotel shortly," Irving told him. "Over dinner we can discuss our travel plans."

"That's fine," Clint said. "I'll stay back here until you come out."

Irving touched Clint's arm and said, "Thank you," then turned and went to his own dressing room.

Clint peered out at the thinning crowd again.

At the back of the theater one man stopped as the rest of the crowd filed past him. He watched the stage carefully, keeping his eyes to the right, and was finally rewarded when he saw Clint Adams's face for just a moment. He and his group hadn't expected that someone like Clint Adams would be the one escorting Irving and Terry around. Adams had moved very quickly earlier that evening, after the shot. He would not be an easy obstacle to overcome.

They were going to need help to get the job done. A lot of help.

Clint kept watching the crowd as they filed out. He was about to withdraw when he thought he saw something. Or someone. A man, standing at the back of the theater, just watching. Then, suddenly, he was gone.

Clint couldn't afford the time to run to the front of the theater. Besides, the man would probably be gone by then, or swallowed up by the departing crowd.

When the theater was empty, he withdrew and walked to where Irving and Terry's dressing rooms were.

EIGHTEEN

Clint decided the safest thing to do was eat in the Gotham's dining room. The cab ride back was quiet, but Ellen Terry was tense the whole time.

When they got out of the cab, Irving asked, "Do you want to go to your room, my dear?"

"No," she said. "I don't want to be alone. And I am hungry."

"So am I," Irving said. He looked at Clint. "I am always famished after a performance."

They went into the hotel, crossed the lobby to the dining room, and were seated. Clint and Irving ordered steak, Ellen Terry chicken.

"So, what did you think?" Irving asked Clint.

"You were very impressive," Clint said. "The both of you."

"You weren't even paying attention," Ellen Terry pointed out.

"I was," Clint said, "part of the time. Most of the time I was watching the audience."

"Which was, of course, more important," Irving said to Terry.

"And what did you see?" Terry asked. "While you were looking at the audience?"

"I saw a lot of people who were being entertained," Clint said, "and, I think, one person who was entertained for a different reason."

"What does that mean?"

"The man who shot at us today?" Irving asked.

"Or somebody working with him."

"So there are two men after us?" Terry asked. "But why?"

"Because," Clint said, "there are men in both our countries who would benefit from some sort of international incident."

"Politicians, most likely," Irving said.

Ellen Terry looked at him.

"You knew this would happen?"

"Let's just say I am not surprised," Irving said.

Clint thought Terry had more to say to the actor, but she was probably going to wait until they were alone.

The waiter came with their meals and they all began to eat with gusto.

"I suggest we leave for Boston tomorrow afternoon," Henry Irving said over dessert. "Would you be able to make those arrangements?"

Clint didn't know when he accepted this assignment to be their bodyguard that he'd also have to play nursemaid and even make the travel arrangements, but he said, "Sure, why not?"

"Not too early, please," Ellen Terry requested.

"Noon should suffice," Irving said.

"Okay. I suppose you'll be taking all your luggage?" he said.

"Why would I leave any of it here?" Terry asked.

That was a good question.

"All right," he said. "I'll make arrangements to have it all picked up and taken to the train. I'll pick both of you up for breakfast, and then we'll go to the train station."

"Maybe," Ellen Terry said, "we could have some policemen on hand to protect us?"

"My dear," Henry said, "that is what we have Clint for. Besides, we don't want to attract too much attention to ourselves."

"We should be okay," Clint said. "Come on. I'll walk you both to your rooms."

NINETEEN

The man approached the heavy oak door and knocked on it. A small window slid open and a pair of eyes looked out. The man held up his hand to exhibit the ring he wore. The window closed, and the door opened.

"Hello, Brother."

"Hello."

"They've gathered in the dining room."

"Thank you."

He knew the way, having been there many times before. He walked down a long hall until he came to a room with an arched ceiling. In the center of the room was a long wooden table with eleven men seated at it. When this man walked to an empty chair and sat down, he made it an even dozen.

The man at the head of the table looked at him and the twelfth man nodded an apology for being late. Actually, he knew he wasn't late at all; he was simply the last to have arrived. Still, an apology was expected.

"Very well," the man at the head of the table said, "we're all here. Let's get started. Henry Irving and Ellen Terry have arrived in New York. They have already performed this evening."

"Why were they allowed to perform?" one man asked. "That was not the plan."

"Plans change," said the man at the head of the table. "Mr. Gray?"

The man who had arrived late—and whose name was not "Mr. Gray"—said, "The United States government has assigned them a bodyguard."

"That was expected," someone said.

"In fact," another man said, "it was assumed."

"Mr. White and Mr. Green are both correct," Mr. Gray said. "However, there was no way we could anticipate who that person would be."

"We assumed they would want to assign their best man," the man at the head of the table said. "We took steps to have James West assigned elsewhere."

"According to plan," Mr. Green pointed out.

"Yes, but what happened next was not according to plan," Mr. Gray said.

"Well," Mr. Red said, "don't keep us in suspense. Who is the bodyguard?"

"His name is Clint Adams," Mr. Gray said.

Silence fell over the table as the men exchanged glances.

"The Gunsmith," Mr. Yellow said.

"Indeed," said Mr. Blue.

Mr. Gray, who was the man who had been standing at the rear of the theater earlier, said, "They have performed and will now be moving on."

“Do we know their schedule?” Mr. Orange asked.

“We assume,” Mr. Gray said, “they will be going to Philadelphia, Washington, and Boston, but we don’t know the correct order.”

“Boston first,” Mr. Blue offered. “It makes sense. North first, and then south to Philadelphia and Washington.”

“And then where?” Mr. Yellow asked.

“West,” Mr. Gray said.

“Perhaps,” the man at the head of the table offered, “it would be better to wait until they are there to take action again.”

“Yes, of course,” Mr. Green said. “Everyone knows how uncivilized the West still is.”

“The law of the gun, and all that,” Mr. White said.

“And with the Gunsmith along,” Mr. Silver said, “no one would be surprised by anything that happened.”

“What about our man in New York?” Mr. Red asked.

“He missed,” the man at the head of the table said. “He will be dealt with.”

“So no one else will be assigned until they go west?” Mr. Gold asked.

“No,” said the man at the head of the table. “But Mr. Gray will accompany them along the way. He will keep in touch with us by telegraph.”

Mr. Gray simply nodded.

“Don’t you think someone should go with him?” Mr. Brown asked.

“I don’t need any help,” Mr. Gray said.

“Not for help,” Mr. Brown said. “For backup.”

“Mr. Gray?” the head man asked.

"No," Mr. Gray said. "I am fine. If I believe I need help, I will send a request."

"All right?" the head man asked, looking up and down the table.

The others in attendance simply nodded.

"Very well," the head man said. "We're adjourned. Mr. Gray, please stay behind for a moment."

Mr. Gray nodded and remained in his seat while the others stood and filed out.

The head man looked down the table at him.

"We need to find someone who is at home in the West," he said. "Someone of Mr. Adams's ilk, who will be able to deal with him."

"Understood, sir."

"Stay in close contact with me," the other man said. "Find out when the actor and actress are leaving New York and let me know."

"Yes, sir."

"And let me know as soon as you find someone."

"Yes, sir."

"You may go."

Mr. Gray got up and started for the door.

"One more thing."

Mr. Gray turned back.

"Yes, sir?"

"In the event you do need help," the other man said, "whom would you prefer I send?"

Mr. Gray thought a moment, then said, "I would prefer Mr. Gold or Mr. Brown."

"Very well," the man at the head of the table said, "Mr. Gold and Mr. Brown. I will be keeping them on standby."

"Yes, sir."

"All right," the man said. "You may go."

Mr. Gray walked back down the hall to the front door, where the man who had allowed him to enter opened the door for him. He stepped outside, and paused to button his coat.

He'd gotten things his way without too much fuss. Now he just had to make sure that things came out the way the group wanted.

The way he wanted.

TWENTY

Clint rose early the next morning and made the travel arrangements for the three of them to Boston. He then sent a telegram to Washington, asking Allan Trehearn to take care of their travel and lodging plans for the remainder of their time in the East. That way, he would no longer have to deal with those tasks.

He met Irving and Terry for breakfast and then had their luggage delivered to the train, which would be leaving at noon.

"What about our hotel?" Ellen Terry asked as they sat in the lobby.

"It's being taken care of," Clint assured her.

"Will it be better than this place?"

"Well, I don't know, Miss Terry," he said. "I guess we'll just have to find out." He looked at Irving. "I'll get us a cab to the train station."

"Very well," Irving said. "We will wait for you right here, Clint."

"Yes, right here, in this spot," Clint said. "Don't move."

He went to the front entrance to talk to the doorman, all the while able to see Irving and Terry in the lobby. When he was done, he rejoined them.

"All right," he said, "we're ready to go."

"I'm not so sure anymore that this whole thing was a very good idea, Henry," Ellen Terry said.

"Don't worry, my dear," Irving said. "Everything will be fine, just fine."

He took her arm and they walked out the front door and into the cab.

Mr. Gray woke that morning with a big-breasted, pale-skinned blond whore lying next to him. He pulled the sheet off her sleeping form so he could look at her. Her large butt was still red, still bore the imprint of his hand. And he could feel the scratches on his own back. Abruptly, he slapped her on the rump again, which woke her with a yelp.

"Hey!" she shouted, reaching back to rub her butt. "Didn't you have enough last night?"

"Not nearly enough," he said. "Turn over."

She rolled onto her back, her big, brown-tipped breasts coming in view. Everything about this girl was big, including her nipples, which was why Mr. Gray had picked her out last night.

He straddled her and attacked her breasts and nipples like a starving man. Meanwhile, his hard cock was trapped between them. After a while he began to rub his cock over her tangle of pubic hair, which scratched his sensitive skin. And eventually, her pussy became moist and began to wet him. Finally, still biting and sucking her nipples, he poked the head of his cock into her slick pussy and drove himself deep into her. She gasped, brought her legs up to wrap them around his waist, and he rode her hard that way until he roared and exploded, then rolled off her . . .

Later, when she got dressed to leave, she commented, "The skin of my nipples is gonna be cracked for a while, from you chewin' on me. You want a woman tonight or tomorrow, you better pick somebody else."

"Don't worry yourself," he said. "I'll be leaving town for a while. By the time I get back, you'll be well healed."

"I hope so," she said. "I'm sore as hell, and I'll be more sore later."

"Here," he said, handing her some extra money, "that's for you. Maybe it'll help you heal."

She smiled at him and rubbed the bills over her chest.

"Yeah," she said, "that'll do the trick."

Mr. Gray got to the train station in time to see Clint Adams board with Henry Irving and Ellen Terry. He waited, giving them time to get seated, then boarded the train himself, but in the car in front of theirs. Once the train started moving, there was no danger that he'd lose them. There was no place to go on a moving train.

Ellen Terry looked around the railroad car at the other passengers, her nose in the air.

"Was it impossible to get us a compartment?" she asked.

"We won't be spending the night on the train," Clint said. "We'll arrive in Boston this evening."

"Yes, well, still . . ."

"Ellen, my dear, you're such a snob," Irving said. "This is all just so wonderfully . . . American."

"Wonderful for you," she muttered, folding her arms and staring out the window.

As they rode the train, both Irving and Ellen Terry dozed off. Clint stayed awake, and to keep himself alert, he read the copy of the *New York Herald* the conductor got for him. On the front page was the story of a woman being killed on the street. She was stabbed several times and her throat was cut. There were no witnesses. The police were looking for anyone who might have information.

Clint noticed that the killing had taken place in the same neighborhood he'd followed Henry Irving to.

A coincidence?

TWENTY-ONE

The performance in Boston went off without a hitch. Irving and Terry got a standing ovation, Clint remained backstage to watch the crowd, but it was a very successful one-day trip, and they were soon on a train to Philadelphia.

They had to take an overnight train out of Boston, so Clint got compartments for both Terry and Irving, while he simply bought himself a seat. He'd slept sitting up many times in the past, and this wouldn't be any hardship.

They ate together in the dining car, and Clint kept a wary eye on all of the other passengers.

"Are we being followed?" Irving asked.

"I don't see anyone," Clint said, "but I wouldn't bet against it. If someone is following us, he's doing a very good job of it."

"That's not very encouraging," Terry said.

"What isn't?" Clint asked.

"That we may have someone following us, and you cannot see him."

"He's probably very good at his job," Clint said.

"And if his job is killing?" she asked.

"If his job was killing, I believe you would be dead by now."

She glared at him.

"So you do not think he's after us to kill us?" Irving asked. "What about the attempt in front of the hotel in New York?"

"If that person was any good, you or I would be dead now," Clint said, "whichever of us was the intended target.

"I think that if we're being followed now, it's probably just to keep track of us. The next attempt will probably be made by a real pro."

"So we have no chance?" Terry demanded. "Is that what you're saying? We are as good as dead?"

"Not at all," Clint said. "I'll do my job, Miss Terry."

"I should hope so!"

She dropped her cloth napkin on the table, stood up, and stormed out, presumably to go back to her compartment.

"She has been very agitated since we left England," Irving said. "Even taking into account how high-strung actresses are, I cannot quite explain it."

"Maybe it's just something about me," Clint said.

"Perhaps, although I myself do not find anything about you annoying. I'm very pleased to have you accompanying us on this tour, and have every confidence that you will do your best to keep us safe."

"Thank you, Henry," Clint said. "When we get to

Philadelphia, I'll send out some telegrams and try to find out if anyone I know has been hired for this job."

"Do you mean to say that you are acquainted with the kind of men who might take a job of killing someone?"

"I'm acquainted with some of them, yes," Clint said. "Some I know by reputation, others personally."

"Remarkable," Irving said.

"You're personally acquainted with other actors, aren't you?" Clint asked.

"Yes, but the only killing any of them do is when they critique someone else's performance."

"Well, there you go, we sometimes critique each other's performances. If someone I know has been hired to kill you, then you can be sure I'll give him my 'critique.' I'll also try to find out who employed him. Like actors, gunmen are usually paid by someone else to perform. And they often know one another."

"Ah, you're speaking of a fraternity of the gun, then?" Irving asked. "Men who share a similar expertise in marksmanship."

"Exactly."

"I see," Irving said. "Well then, hopefully someone in your fraternity will know something."

"That's the hope," Clint said.

"Why don't we get some more coffee?" Irving suggested, and looked around for a waiter.

Mr. Gray watched from between the cars as Clint Adams and Henry Irving ordered more coffee. He was hungry, and waiting for them to leave the dining car so he could go in and have something to eat. He did not want to take the chance of Adams seeing him, and possibly remembering him later. He was starting to think he needed at least one more person to be able to keep watch properly, and safely. When he got to Philadelphia, he'd send a telegram to ask for Mr. Green or Mr. Gold to meet them in Washington D.C. before they headed west.

He pressed his forehead to the glass window while watching Adams and Irving drink their fresh coffee. Perhaps when they were done, they'd leave the car and he could get something to quiet the hunger pangs in his stomach.

TWENTY-TWO

Philadelphia was as successful as Boston had been, if not more so. A standing ovation again, including several members of local government. From there they rode the train to Washington D.C. It was the shorter of the three train trips.

When they arrived, they took a cab to the Georgetown Hotel. It was one of the best hotels in the city, and satisfied Ellen Terry much more than the hotels in New York, Boston, or Philadelphia.

"Now this is more like it," she said as they entered her opulent suite. "This is a room befitting my status."

"I'm glad you're satisfied," Clint said. "Come on, Henry. Your turn."

Irving looked at Terry and said, "We will be back to pick you up for the performance."

"What about eating?" she asked.

Irving looked at his watch and said, "That will have to wait until after."

At that moment a bellman appeared carrying a basket of fruit.

"Compliments of the house for Miss Terry," he said.

"Put it down over there," Terry said. "At least I won't starve."

"Come on, Henry."

Clint hustled the bellman out of Terry's room, then walked Irving down the hall to his own. It was a suite that matched Terry's.

"Thank you," Irving said. "I guess I don't rate the same basket of fruit Ellen received."

"I can have one sent up."

"Not necessary," Irving said. "I'm going to take a bath and get ready for tonight's performance."

"All right," Clint said. "I'll be in my room further down the hall."

Clint left and walked to his room. He entered and saw that his was more conventional, containing a bed, a chest of drawers, some chairs, and a writing desk. As with the suites Irving and Terry had, there was running water.

He dropped his carpetbag on the bed and walked to his window to look out. He was in the rear of the hotel, so his view was of the street behind the hotel.

He was about to open his bag when there was a knock at the door. He expected either Irving or Terry with a complaint. Still he answered the door with his hand on the Colt New Line behind his back. The gun and holster were in his bag.

When he opened the door, he saw neither the actor nor the actress. It was Allan Trehearn.

"Mr. Adams," Trehearn said. "May I come in?"

"Why not?" Clint asked. "After all, you're paying for the rooms."

"Not me," Trehearn said, entering, "the government."

"At the moment, it's the same thing to me," Clint said, closing the door. "What's on your mind?"

"We understand there was an attempt on Henry Irving's life in New York."

"That was days ago," Clint said, "and it might just as well have been an attempt on me. We don't know for sure."

"What about Boston and Philadelphia?" Trehearn asked. "How did it go there?"

"No problems," Clint said.

"Are you being followed? Watched?"

"I don't doubt it, but I haven't been able to spot anyone."

Trehearn rubbed his jaw thoughtfully.

"Maybe you need help."

"If I do," Clint said, "I'll get it. I'm going to be sending telegrams to friends to try and get some information."

"About what?"

"About who might have been hired for this job," Clint said.

"If you know someone who can tell you that, it's a pretty good contact to have."

"And what about your contacts?" Clint asked. "What do they tell you? Has anyone else come across from England, maybe with an eye toward harming the two national treasures?"

"As far as we've discovered, no," Trehearn said. "Of course, that doesn't mean someone didn't manage to come over on a boat—we just don't know about it."

"Very encouraging."

"How are you getting along with them?"

"Fine, with Irving," Clint said. "The woman, Terry, is very hard to satisfy."

"Is there anything I can do for you?"

"Yes," Clint said. "I need a Boston newspaper and a Philadelphia newspaper for the days following the performances."

"Looking for reviews?"

"Something like that."

"Okay, I'll see what I can do."

"Try to have them here tonight when we get back from the theater."

"I'll do my best."

Clint let Trehearn out and closed the door behind him. He had tried to keep an eye on Irving while they were in Boston and Philadelphia, but he couldn't sit awake all night. The actor could have gotten out of the hotel at night to go for a walk, like the one he'd taken in New York.

Of course, that didn't make him a killer, but it would be real interesting if there were murders in Boston and Philadelphia similar to the one in New York.

Clint wondered if there were any similar murders in London before Irving and Terry left. He'd have to ask Trehearn to get him a London newspaper as well.

Clint didn't really think Henry Irving was a killer, but it was an odd coincidence that he'd taken a walk in New York in the same area as the murder.

And of all the coincidences he hated, he hated the odd ones the most.

TWENTY-THREE

Clint watched the performance from backstage again. As with the other stops, Washington D.C. appreciated everything Henry Irving and Ellen Terry had to offer. The audience gave them a standing ovation, and demanded an encore. Luckily, Irving and Terry had plenty of material.

Before leaving for the theater, Clint went to a telegraph office and sent off his questions. He knew a few people around the country—Rick Hartman in Texas, Talbot Roper in Denver, Duke Farrell in San Francisco—who would be able to answer him. If they knew anything. He hoped to have replies by morning, before they were scheduled to leave Washington.

Afterward Clint watched the house empty out while Irving and Terry changed into their street clothes. As in Boston and Philadelphia, he did not see anyone paying any special attention from the back of the theater, but he still had the feeling somebody was out there.

"Clint?"

He turned, saw Irving standing there in his suit. He was carrying his walking stick, and wearing his top hot.

"Do you always dress like this?" Clint asked.

Irving looked down at himself.

"Well," he said, "on performance night, usually. Why?" Irving looked again. "Don't you like it?"

"It's nice," Clint said. "Real nice."

"Well," Irving said, "Ellen is ready to go to dinner."

"Okay. Hotel dining room okay?"

"For once, yes," Irving said. "She thinks it will be very good, if the quality matches her suite."

"Good," Clint said. "I certainly want Miss Terry to be satisfied."

He took one last look at the empty house, then turned and walked with Irving.

"They're very good," Mr. Green said.

"Yes, they are," Mr. Gray said.

"Was that Adams backstage? Kept peering out?" Mr. Green asked.

"Yes," Mr. Gray said. "He watches all the performances from there."

"Has he seen you yet?"

"I think he saw me in New York," Mr. Gray said, "but not since we left there."

"Where do they usually go after the theater?" Mr. Green asked.

"To dinner," Mr. Gray said. "They'll probably go to the hotel dining room."

"How do you usually play it?"

"I usually follow behind them," Mr. Gray said. "If we both do it, though, they'll spot us."

"So what do you suggest?"

"You go ahead to the hotel and wait there."

"What if they don't go there?"

"Then I will follow them whenever they go," Mr. Gray said. "Eventually, they will return to the hotel."

Mr. Green shrugged and said, "Okay, it's your call."

Mr. Gray chose not to read anything into his colleague's tone. After all, it was his call.

Clint and Irving ordered steak dinners; Terry went with her usual chicken. Henry Irving ordered a bottle of wine for them.

"You know, my dear," Irving said to her, "when we travel out West, you might have to eat steak. It's what they eat in the West."

"I will deal with that situation when it arises," Terry said.

"Isn't that true?" Irving asked Clint.

"Pretty much," Clint said. "Steak, beef, but I'll bet she can get some chicken. Maybe even some fish."

"Freshwater fish, correct?" Irving asked.

"Oh, yeah," Clint said. "Not much ocean fish between here and California."

"Trout?" Irving asked.

"Lots of them."

"Catfish?"

"What do you know of catfish, Henry?" Terry asked.

"Not much," Henry said, "but I'd like to taste it."

"When we get to Saint Louis," Clint said, "you will."

"Excellent."

"But we have a couple of stops before that."

"Small stops," Henry said.

"Nothing small about Chicago, Henry," Clint said.

"I am looking forward to Chicago," Ellen Terry said. "I've heard a lot about it. I hope it's all true."

"We will see," Henry Irving said.

After dinner they all went to their rooms. Clint was reading when there was a knock at his door. A bellman, perhaps with a message. Or maybe Henry Irving.

When he opened the door, it was Trehearn again. The government man held out the newspapers in his hand.

"The papers you requested," he said.

"Thank you."

"Run out of books to read?"

"Just wanted some light reading as well," Clint said. "Thank you."

"Is there anything else you need while you're in Washington?" Trehearn asked.

"No, nothing."

"Stay in touch, then."

"I will."

He closed the door, heard Trehearn's footsteps receding down the hall. He turned, walked back to the chair he had been sitting in, moved the book he'd been reading, and sat down. He read the Boston newspaper first, then the Philadelphia. In the Boston paper there was a story on page five about a street whore being killed—stabbed. In the Philadelphia paper a similar story appeared on page one. That was a good example of the differences between the two cities.

Three U.S. cities visited by Henry Irving, three dead

women. Had Irving gone for walks in all three cities? Or just New York?

He put the newspapers down and left his room. He walked down the hall and knocked on Irving's door. The actor answered.

"Ah, Clint. What brings you to my door this late?" the actor asked.

"I was just checking on you," Clint said. "To make sure you're all right."

"I'm quite fine," Irving said. "Would you like to come in for a drink?"

"No, thanks," Clint said. "I'm going to turn in. Good night."

"Good night, then."

Irving closed his door, and Clint started walking back to his room. But as he passed Ellen Terry's door, it opened. She appeared in the doorway, wearing a silk dressing gown that molded itself to her body. It was obvious she was wearing nothing beneath it.

"What's happening out here?"

"Nothing," Clint said. "I was just checking to see if Henry was in for the night."

"And is he?"

"He is."

"And were you going to check on me?"

"I was."

"But you were walking past my door, were you not?" she asked.

"Was I?"

"I believe you were."

"Well, if I was, it was only because I didn't want to disturb you."

"What if I want to be disturbed?"

"Excuse me?"

"I want to have a nightcap, Mr. Adams," she said, "and I don't want to have it alone. Will you have one with me?"

"If that's what you want, Miss Terry."

"Come in, then," she said. "And close the door behind you."

She turned and went into the room. Clint entered and closed the door, as instructed.

"The wine is over there," she said, pointing.

Clint walked to the far end of her suite and poured two glasses of wine. He walked back to where she was standing, and handed one to her.

"Thank you."

"You're welcome."

"Have a seat," she said. "Let's talk."

"About what?"

"Anything," she said. "I am not sleepy, and I need to talk."

"All right," he said, taking a seat, "let's talk."

TWENTY-FOUR

"Tell me about Henry," Clint said.

She sat across from him, in the plush armchair that was the twin to his.

"That's what you want to talk about?"

"Yes."

She sipped her wine and shrugged.

"Very well. What do you want to know?"

"What does he do when he's not on stage?"

"He manages the theater, reads plays. He plans what he will do when he is on stage."

"That's all?"

"What else is there?"

"For instance. Does he have any hobbies?"

"Hobbies?" Terry laughed. "Like what?"

"Does he . . . take walks? At night?"

"Walks?"

"Yes," Clint said. "Some people like to walk. It clears their head."

"Henry's head is always clear."

"So he always knows what he's doing?"

"Oh, yes," she said. "He is always very clear on what he is doing."

"What about you, Miss Terry?" Clint asked. "Are you always clear on what you're doing?"

"Usually."

"What is it about me that upsets you so much?" Clint asked.

"You know," she said, "I've been wondering about that myself. What is it about you that irritates me?"

"I'd like to know the answer to that."

She put her glass down, stood up, and approached him. She stopped about a foot in front of him. He could see the outline of her nipples beneath the silk.

"You're supposed to see to my every need while we're here, isn't that right?" she asked.

"That's right."

She took his glass from his hand and set it aside on a nearby table. Then she spread her legs and dropped down into his lap. Her weight was pleasant as she leaned forward and kissed him. That was even more pleasant. It went on for a while. He put his hands on her thighs, felt the warmth of her skin through the silk.

She cupped his face in her hands and sat back.

"Open my robe," she told him.

He did. Her breasts were small, but her skin was flawless and pale, her nipples pink.

"This is why you annoyed me," she said. "Because I wanted you."

"Wanted?"

"Want," she said, "still."

"And that bothers you?"

"You're an uneducated American, and a Westerner," she said. "You're not my equal."

"You think not?"

She stroked her own breast with her hand, cupped his chin with the other.

"Do you want to prove me wrong?" she asked.

"I think we're talking about it too much," he said. He stood up, lifting her in his arms. He carried her to the next room, set her down on the bed. Then he peeled her robe off, flipping her as he did so, removing it and tossing it to the floor.

She was naked on the bed, the tangled hair between her legs as auburn as the hair on her head. He stroked her breasts, her belly, her flanks. Her nostrils flared as she bit her lip. His hand moved between her legs, probed, came away wet. He lifted his fingers to his nose for a sniff, then licked them.

"Oh, my . . ." she said. "You're a nasty man. I knew it."

He reached for her again, but she closed her thighs tightly.

"Undress," she said. "You can't touch me again until you are naked."

"Have it your way, my lady."

He stepped back, began to undress. He set his gun down on the night table, within easy reach.

"Are you ever without a gun?" she asked.

"Never," he said, taking off his boots.

"Why not?"

"If I'm ever caught without a gun, I'm a dead man," he said, stripping off his shirt.

"Who wants to kill you?"

"Every young pup who thinks he's good with a gun," he said, removing his britches. Now he was naked.

"Oh my," she said, taking in his naked body, "you are a lovely man."

"Thank you." His cock stood straight up, swelled by the feel of her in his lap, and the smell of her on his fingers.

"Come here."

He moved closer to the bed. Lying on her back, she reached out and took him with one hand, stroked him so that he swelled even more. A bead of liquid appeared on the head of his cock. She smeared it with her fingers, then lifted them to her nose to sniff, and her mouth to lick.

"See?" she said. "I can be as nasty as you."

"And here I thought you were a lady," Clint said.

"Oh, I am," she said. "On stage, in public, I am ever the lady. But here, in my bedroom, I'm a whore, like most women."

She reached for him again and continued to stroke him. Then she tightened her hand and pulled him.

"Come," she said, "on the bed with me."

He climbed into the bed beside her. She moved over to allow him room, and turned to face him. He kissed her, stroking her again, her thigh, her ass, her back. She held tight to his cock, which was now between them.

"I hope," she whispered against his mouth, "that you are ready to give a command performance tonight, Clint Adams."

"I'll certainly do my best," Clint answered, "my lady."

TWENTY-FIVE

Henry Irving pulled on his dress trousers, then his boots, shined until they reflected light. He was wearing a fresh white shirt. He stood, reached for his black jacket, and donned it. He looked at himself in the mirror and nodded. Next he took up his top hat and set it atop his head as a rakish angle, attached his black cape, then picked up his silver-tipped walking stick.

Time for another late-night walk.

As Irving left the hotel, Mr. Green said, "There's the actor."

"Indeed," Mr. Gray said.

"Where's he going?"

"I don't know."

"We should follow him," Mr. Green said.

"He'll be back."

"But . . . we might have a chance to kill him," Mr. Green argued.

"Not here," Mr. Gray said.

"What do you mean?"

"Not in Washington."

"Why not?"

"It will look better if he's killed in the West," Mr. Gray said. "By some crazed gunman."

"But this is our chance—"

"And what about the actress?" Mr. Gray asked. "If we kill the actor tonight, the actress will go back to England."

Mr. Green took a moment, then said, "You're probably right."

"I know I am," Mr. Gray said. "You can turn in, Mr. Green. I'll keep watch here."

"Are you sure?"

"Quite sure."

Mr. Green nodded, turned, and walked away into the shadows.

Mr. Gray settled himself in the doorway, leaning, arms folded, and continued to watch the front door of the hotel. He doubted very much that the actress would be coming out before morning. He'd keep watch until the actor came back, and then turn in himself.

TWENTY-SIX

Ellen Terry pushed Clint down onto his back and mounted him. She rode him slowly, up and down, up and down, his hands on her hips, his eyes watching her breasts as they bobbed in front of him.

"Don't move," she said, "just don't move. I want to enjoy this for a while . . ."

"As long as you like, my lady," Clint said.

She opened her eyes and smiled down at him.

"Is that a fact?"

"It is."

"We'll see about that."

She increased the tempo then rode him hard, grinding herself down on him each time she came down. He lifted his hips to her, matching her tempo, confident that he would outlast her, because he'd been with many women before, and he knew his own stamina well.

She began to perspire, and to glisten with it, and finally she fell upon him, exhausted.

"You bastard!" she said, her face against his chest.

"You said a command performance," he reminded her.

"Yes, I did," she said. "I just need . . . to rest."

"Well," he said, "I don't."

He grabbed her, flipped her onto her back, and mounted her.

"Wha—"

"Quiet!"

He used his knees to spread her thighs, then drove his hard cock into her. She gasped, her eyes going wide then closing.

"Oh, God," she said as he fucked her, taking her hard and fast.

He slid his hands beneath her smooth ass, gripped it tightly enough that he knew he'd leave finger marks on her. She wrapped her legs around him and held on to him with her arms, her nails raking his back.

Her breath came in gasps as he took her, grunting as he drove into her. The room filled with the mingled scent of their sex and sweat, with the sounds of their grunts and groans.

Clint knew this night that if he had an audience, he'd be earning his own standing ovation.

Mr. Gray straightened and dropped his arms to his sides. Henry Irving was coming back down the street, two hours after he left. Mr. Gray watched as Irving walked with a bounce in his step, obviously pleased with whatever he had done or seen during his walk.

The actor exchanged a greeting with the doorman

and entered the hotel. It was so late Mr. Gray felt sure Irving would go to his room and go to bed.

That was what he intended to do.

Ellen Terry lay on her side, her knees drawn up to her chest.

"You're wearing me out," she said.

"I thought that was the point," Clint said. "Or am I wrong?"

She stole a look at him over her shoulder. He was lying behind her, admiring her smooth ass.

"The point was for me to exhaust you," she said.

"Well," he said, "I'm sorry if I disappointed you."

"I didn't say I was disappointed," she said, "just exhausted. Let's get some sleep."

"All right." He started to get up from the bed.

"Where are you going?" she asked.

"You said you wanted us to go to sleep. I'm going to my room."

"I want you to sleep here," she said. "I may be tired, but I'm not finished with you yet."

He got back into bed.

"I just need a couple of hours of sleep," she said, cuddling up to him.

She closed her eyes and was asleep almost immediately.

Clint figured this was a good way to secure Ellen Terry's safety. On the other hand, Henry Irving could have been out roaming the streets, even though he'd been in his room when Clint checked.

He closed his eyes. It would probably be easier to

keep an eye on them when they went west, where he was more at home.

He closed his eyes and went to sleep.

Ellen Terry woke him twice during the night and they went at it again. She still insisted on trying to exhaust him, but only succeeded in exhausting herself. Finally, she fell asleep for the rest of the night, which he appreciated.

He was much more tired than he wanted her to know.

TWENTY-SEVEN

In the morning, Clint slipped from the bed without waking Terry and went to his own room. He washed and dressed, went down to the front desk to see if any replies had come in from his telegrams.

"Yes, sir," the clerk said. "We sent a bellman to your room, but there was no answer."

"I'm a sound sleeper," Clint said. He accepted the telegrams the clerk gave him.

It was 8:30 a.m. They had a 2 p.m. train to catch, which left plenty of time for breakfast, time to read the telegrams and, perhaps, a local newspaper.

He went to the dining room and got a table for four, just in case Irving or Terry came down.

"Steak and eggs," he told the waiter, "and a newspaper, please."

"Yes, sir," the waiter said. "Comin' up."

Drinking coffee, he read the telegrams. His three friends had all responded, but to no avail. They hadn't heard a word of a hired killer taking a job to kill two visiting actors from England. Each promised they would keep their ears open and report to him when they heard anything.

He folded the telegrams and put them in his pocket. His breakfast came and he started to eat. As he did, Henry Irving came walking into the dining room.

"Ah," he said, "I thought I was the first to awaken. May I join you?"

"Of course."

Irving sat down and told the waiter, "I would like some . . . what do you call them here . . . oh yes, some flapjacks."

"Comin' up, sir," the waiter said.

"Thank you."

Irving poured himself some coffee, looked across the table at Clint.

"How did you sleep?"

"I had a very . . . satisfactory night," Clint said.

"Good, good," Irving said. "I slept soundly myself."

"That's good," Clint said.

When the waiter brought Irving his breakfast, he also brought a newspaper for Clint.

"Hot off the presses, sir."

"Thanks."

Clint spread the paper and saw the story right away. A woman killed on the streets—stabbed.

Could he accuse Henry Irving simply because the man liked to take walks? Had he taken a walk last night? He decided to broach the subject as a curiosity.

"This is strange," he said.

"What's that?" Irving asked.

"This story in the newspaper." Clint folded the paper so that it featured the story of the murdered girl, and then passed the newspaper to the actor.

Irving scanned the story, his face impassive, and then passed the paper back to Clint.

"Terrible, terrible thing," he said.

"I've noticed," Clint said, "that this sort of thing is happening quite a bit here in the East. Boston, Philadelphia, and now Washington."

"All of the cities we've performed in," Irving pointed out. "Yes, that's very odd."

The waiter came and set Irving's flapjacks down in front of him. The actor covered them with copious amounts of maple syrup and dug in.

"You know," Clint said, "I thought I noticed you going out for a walk one night. Was it Boston? Or when we were in New York?"

"Probably all of them," Irving said. He picked up a napkin and wiped maple syrup from his face. "I often go for walks at night."

"I wonder if you were anywhere near these locations," Clint said.

"If I was," Irving said, "I didn't see or hear anything. Quite a shame. Perhaps I could have been of some assistance to these poor women. Or even to the police."

"That's true."

Irving looked at the door.

"Ellen should come down and have breakfast," Irving said. "We must get ready for our train."

"It doesn't leave until two," Clint said. "We have time."

"I knocked on her door as I passed. She didn't answer, but perhaps I managed to wake her."

"Well, if she doesn't come down soon, we'll have to go and get her."

They were finishing their breakfast when the desk clerk suddenly appeared at their table.

"Excuse me, sirs."

They both looked up at him.

"Yes?"

"There's a policeman in the lobby. He would like to come in and talk to you."

"To me?" Clint asked.

"No, sir," the clerk said, "to Mr. Irving."

"A policeman?" Irving asked. "Whatever for?"

"I—I don't know, sir," the clerk said. "He asked for you, and I told him you were in here. He asked me to come in and ask if you would like to come out, or should he come in?"

Irving looked at Clint, who simply shrugged. He could think of only one reason a policeman would want to talk to the actor. Maybe somebody saw him during his walk the night before.

How would he explain it to Trehearn and the two governments if Henry Irving was arrested for murder?

"By all means," Irving said, "let the gentleman enter. The least we can do is offer him a cup of coffee."

"Yes, sir," the clerk said. "I'll tell him."

As the clerk left, Irving looked across the table at Clint once again.

"What can this be about?" he said.

"Damned if I know," Clint replied as another man entered the dining room, "but we're about to find out."

TWENTY-EIGHT

The man approached the table, a bowler hat in his hand. He wore a gray suit, had a large, carefully manicured mustache, and a shock of gray hair.

"Mr. Irving. Sir?" the man asked.

"Yes, sir," Irving said. "How can I help you?"

"Uh, sir . . ." The policeman looked curiously at Clint.

"My name is Clint Adams," he said as the man studied him.

"Oh, yes, sir," the man said. "I'm Inspector Lester."

"Inspector," Irving said, "why don't you sit down and join us. May we offer you some coffee?"

"Coffee would be good," the inspector said. "I've been up most of the night."

"And is that what brings you here this morning?" Irving asked, pouring the policeman a cup of coffee while the man seated himself.

"Yes, sir. It is. Thank you." He picked up the coffee and sipped it gratefully.

"Why don't we get you some breakfast as well?" Irving offered.

"I am hungry, but no thank you, sir. That will have to wait, I'm afraid."

"All right, then," Irving said. "Why don't you tell us what is on your mind?"

"Well, there was a murder on the streets last night," the inspector said. "A young woman was stabbed to death."

"Yes," Irving said, "we read about it in the newspaper."

"It made the newspaper already?" Lester asked. "That was fast. Well, this is Washington. Word gets around very fast."

"But what brings you here, to talk to Henry?" Clint asked.

"Ah, well," Lester said, "we have a witness who described the killer."

"How fortunate," Irving said.

"Oh, they can't identify him. Didn't see his face. But they did describe how he was dressed. He wore a dark suit, a cape, a top hat, and carried a cane."

"Ah," Irving said, "your killer seems to have similar tastes in attire to me."

"Yes," the inspector said, "that's what brings me here. Someone saw you going out last night for a walk, dressed that way."

"Who would that have been?" Clint asked. "Who saw him and got the information to you so fast?"

"I can't say," the inspector said. "But I did want to

come and ask you, sir, about your whereabouts last night."

"I went for a walk, and then I was in my room," Irving said.

"What time did you go for a walk?"

"Oh, it was quite late," Irving said. "It was after Clint came by my room to check on me."

"What time was that?" Lester looked at both men.

"After ten," Clint said.

"And did you go for a walk immediately after that, sir?" Lester asked.

"Not immediately, no," Irving said. "I think it was about an hour later."

"So . . . around eleven p.m.?"

"After eleven p.m.," Irving said.

"Uh-huh . . ."

"What did your witness say?" Clint asked.

"I told you," Lester said, "he didn't see much—"

"No, I mean the witness who told you about Mr. Irving's walk," Clint said. "It must have been either the desk clerk or the doorman, right?"

Lester looked into his coffee cup.

Clint looked at Irving and said, "Probably the doorman."

"I did exchange pleasantries with the man on the way out and on the way in."

"And when he heard about the murder, and the witness's description, he sent for the police right away."

"And the inspector appeared," Irving said.

"So," Inspector Lester said, "am I to understand you didn't see or hear anything while you were . . . out walking?"

"I did not."

"And need I ask," the inspector said, "did you kill the woman?"

"I did not."

The inspector looked at Clint.

"I know who you are."

"Do you?"

"Oh, yes," Lester said. "You're a very famous man, Mr. Adams. Everybody knows who you are, but the legend of the Gunsmith lives in the West, not here in the East."

Clint didn't respond.

Lester looked at Henry Irving.

"When will you be leaving?" he asked.

"This afternoon."

"I hope," Lester said, standing, "no other girls get killed before you leave."

"Actually," Irving said, "I hope one does after I leave."

"Sir?" Lester seemed taken aback.

"If a woman is killed after I leave, that will prove I had nothing to do with the first one, wouldn't it?" Irving asked.

"Yes, I suppose it would," Lester said. "Where will you go from here?"

"Many cities and towns across the West," Irving said. "We have quite a long schedule ahead of us."

"Well," Inspector Lester said, "I'll be watching your progress."

"I'm sure you'll find other more important things to occupy your time, Inspector."

Lester looked at them both, said, "Gentlemen," and left.

"So," Irving said.

"So what?"

"Do you also suspect me of killing these women?" the actor asked.

"The thought had crossed my mind."

"And now?"

"I don't know," Clint said. "I guess we'll just have to see."

Irving reached out and picked up the newspaper again, looked at the story.

"Women in Philadelphia and Boston as well?"

"Yes."

"New York?"

"Yes."

Irving put down the newspaper.

"Only one in each city?"

"Yes."

Irving helped himself to more coffee, then poured more maple syrup on the remainder of his flapjacks.

"I suppose, given the evidence, I might suspect me as well."

"It would be helpful," Clint said, "if no other women turned up murdered during our travels."

Irving speared a huge chunk of syrupy flapjack and, prior to stuffing it into his mouth, said, "I will keep that in mind."

TWENTY-NINE

While Irving went to his room to pack, Clint knocked on Ellen Terry's door. She opened it, wearing the same silk robe as the night before.

"You bastard," she said. "My legs are like rubber."

"Is that why you didn't come down for breakfast?" he asked.

"I have packing to do," she said.

"Are you hungry?"

"Starving."

"I'll have something brought up," Clint said. "What would you like?"

"Surprise me."

"I thought I did that last night."

She smiled and said, "No, none of that was a surprise."

"I'll see to your breakfast," he said. "You better finish your packing. We won't want to miss our train this afternoon."

"We won't miss it," she said.

He nodded, went back downstairs to see to her breakfast.

Across the street, Mr. Green watched as the policeman entered the hotel then left later on. He knew the inspector because he had been to Washington D.C. before.

"What's going on?" Mr. Gray asked, coming up alongside his colleague.

"The police have been here."

"How do you know that?"

"See that man getting into the carriage? Inspector Lester."

"And how do you know that?"

"I've been here before."

"I didn't know that," Mr. Gray said. "Why was he here?"

"I'm guessing it has something to do with the woman who was killed last night."

"What woman?"

"A whore, probably," Mr. Green said. "She was stabbed on the street."

"What's that got to do with us?"

"I went into the lobby and took a peek. The inspector was sitting with Adams and the actor."

"Why question them?"

"He must have suspected one of them," Mr. Green said. "Maybe the actor."

"Why?"

"There was a girl killed in New York as well," Mr. Green said. "It was in the newspaper."

"What about Boston, and Philadelphia?"

"We can check."

"So you think the actor is a killer of women?"

"You said he went for a walk."

"That doesn't mean he killed anybody."

"I guess we'll have to wait and see," Mr. Green said. "If he has a taste for it, it will happen again. And again."

"You're probably right."

"They're leaving this afternoon," Mr. Gray said. "You can go, but meet me at the train station at one."

"I'll be there."

They exchanged places in the doorway.

"Are we going west with them?" Mr. Green asked.

"We're going west."

"I've never been west," Mr. Green said. "This will be interesting."

THIRTY

Ellen Terry had her breakfast and got dressed. Clint had a bellman go to each room and bring the luggage downstairs, where the bags were loaded on a wagon and taken to the train station.

Clint, Irving, and Terry rode there in a different carriage.

"I am sensing a change in the weather," Henry Irving said.

"What kind of change?" Terry asked. "The weather seems the same to me."

"It was a metaphor, my lady," Irving said, giving them both a knowing look.

"Oh, shut up, Henry," Terry said.

"Far be it from me to pass judgment," he said. "Not when I myself am suspected of murder."

"What are you babbling about?" she asked. "What part are you playing now?"

"I'll explain it to you," Clint said, "when we get on the train."

True to his word, Clint explained everything about the dead girls to Ellen Terry when they were on the train. They were sitting in the passenger car, even though they had compartments reserved for the trek west. The first stop would be Chicago, Illinois.

Clint didn't know how fast the train was going to go. He knew that trains could run at 20 miles an hour a lot cheaper than at 30, and to railway companies, saving money was paramount. It was going to take them at least 30 hours, plus the time for stops. He figured 36 hours for the whole trip. A lot could happen in 36 hours.

"That's horrible," Ellen Terry said when he was done.

"The poor girls," Irving said.

"No," she said, "I mean it's terrible that the policeman in Washington actually suspected Henry of those murders. That's preposterous."

"The man was doing his job," Irving said.

"So was the doorman," Clint said, "when he sent for a policeman."

Terry looked at Clint.

"You're supporting what that policeman did?" she asked.

"I'm supporting what he did," Clint said, "but not what he thought."

"Then you don't believe that Henry is a killer?" she asked.

Clint looked at Irving, who was waiting for the answer.

"No," Clint said, "I don't believe it."

"Well," Terry said, "that's good."

"I think we ought to move you to your compartments," Clint said. "Get settled, and then we'll go to the dining car for something to eat. All right?"

"Whatever you say, Clint," Terry said. "You are the boss, right?"

Clint looked at Irving, who shrugged.

"That's right," Clint said. "I'm the boss."

He walked Irving to his compartment, and then Terry to hers. She stepped inside, then grabbed the front of his shirt and pulled him in. She wrapped her arms around him and kissed him soundly. He returned the kiss, but then broke away.

"Ellen, we can't do this now," he said.

"Why not?"

"I have to check out the entire train," Clint said, "before we go and get something to eat. Now you lock this door and keep it locked unless it's Henry or me. Understand?"

"Of course I understand," she said. "I am an educated woman, not one of those backwoods females you are used to dealing with."

"Okay, then," he said. "I'll be back in a little while."

"Return quickly," she said. "I'll be hungry in that little while."

"Yeah," he said. "So will I."

He stepped out into the all, slid the door closed, and waited until he heard it lock.

THIRTY-ONE

Clint went in search of the conductor, found him in one of the passenger cars.

"Mind if I talk to you a minute?"

"Yes, sir," the man said.

"Outside?"

They stepped out between two passenger cars. The conductor was an old-timer, sixty if he was a day, white-haired and pale-skinned.

Clint told the man who he was and what he was doing on the train.

"You're serious?" the conductor asked. "We got two famous people on board?"

"Very famous," Clint said. "And it's my job to keep them safe."

"Can I help?"

"Maybe," Clint said. "What's your name?"

"Al Sykes."

"Well, Al," Clint said, "I'm going to walk the train and take a look at all the passengers."

"Lookin' for somebody suspicious?" the conductor asked, lowering his voice.

"That's right," Clint said. "What I need to know from you is, are there any other people on the train that aren't in the passenger cars and compartments?"

"Well," Sykes said, taking off his hat and scratching his head, "other than the other conductor, Ben, the cooks and waiters in the dining car, and the engineer and fireman, nope."

"Nobody in the stock car?"

"Well, yeah, we got one man in there watching the animals."

"See, that's what I mean, Al. Anybody else?"

The man thought a minute, then said, "No. Nobody else."

"Good. Then I'm going to start walking. If I need your help, I'll let you know, okay?"

"Sure thing, mister . . ."

"Just call me Clint."

"Okay, Clint."

"Then let's both go back to work." Clint shook the man's hand, and they both returned to the forward passenger car.

THIRTY-TWO

Clint walked the passenger cars one at a time, studying the people. Nobody immediately jumped out at him as suspicious, but there were plenty of men traveling alone, or by twos, that he'd keep an eye on. He discounted the people who were traveling with women and children as being possible problems.

When he was done, he found Sykes and had him introduce him to all the people who worked on the train. Sykes took him and introduced him to the engine crew, and then the kitchen and dining car crew. After that, he met the other conductor—a younger man named Henry—and finally the man in the stock car, Teddy, who was a wrangler of sorts.

Finally convinced he'd seen everybody on the train in under two hours, he went back to get Henry Irving and Ellen Terry and take them to the dining car.

He knocked on Irving's door first, and then when

Ellen Terry opened hers and saw both of them, she seemed disappointed. She had probably been hoping Clint would return alone.

"Two gentlemen to escort you to the dining car, madam," Henry Irving said.

"Well, aren't I the lucky girl?" she said sweetly.

They walked to the dining car and were seated, Irving and Terry on one side, Clint on the other. A black waiter wearing a white jacket and white gloves came and took their order.

"See any murderers on board?" Terry asked.

"No obvious ones," Clint said. "But they could be all around us."

"That is not funny," she said.

"It wasn't meant to be," Clint said. "I just want you to be aware that we have to be careful at all times."

"Well then," she said, "maybe you should keep a very close eye on me."

"And me as well," Irving offered, not getting what Ellen Terry was referring to.

"I'll keep a close eye on both of you. Don't worry." Clint looked at Irving. "Henry, I don't think you should go for any more late-night walks. Especially not in a city like Chicago."

"They help me sleep," Irving said, "but all right, Clint. I'll do as you wish."

"And you," Clint said to Terry.

"What about me?"

"You're going to have to stay in your room."

"In case you haven't noticed," she said, "that's what I have been doing. The only time I leave is to perform, or eat with you."

"Fine," Clint said. "We'll keep it that way."

The waiter came with their food and they ate while staring out the window and talking about what was going by. In some stretches, Ellen Terry said she could almost think they were riding a British railway.

"It looks the same," she said, "in some places. But all in all, I can't wait to go home."

"We have a lot of time left on this tour, my dear," Irving said.

"I know that," she said. "And I'll fulfill my part of the bargain." She looked at Clint. "Have you ever been to England?"

He nodded. "I was in London, for a gun expo, years ago. Nice city."

"Nice?" she asked. "It is the greatest city in the world. Restaurants, museums, theater—oh, the theater. You should come again so I can show you around."

"I'll keep that in mind," Clint said.

They finished eating and Clint walked them back to their compartments. He wanted to drop Terry off first, but they passed Irving's door before hers, and it would have looked suspicious, like he was trying to avoid being at her door without Irving.

"I'm right down the hall," he told Irving. "If you want anything at all, ask me, nobody else. Not even the conductor."

"I understand."

They closed his door, and walked to Terry's. She stepped inside, then turned to face him.

"Are you coming in?"

"Not yet," he said. "I've still got some work to do.

And if Henry looks for me, I want him to be able to find me."

"And tonight?" she asked. "When everyone else is asleep?"

He stepped in long enough to take her in his arms and kiss her, then he released her and backed out again.

With a smile, he said, "Well, that's another story, isn't it?"

THIRTY-THREE

Chicago went perfectly.

They played the Globe Theater and, as with the other performances, commanded standing ovations. Unlike the other locations, Irving and Terry were given a party afterward, a party that was supposed to include the mayor on its guest list. Instead, they sent a representative of the mayor's office, a low-level assistant.

By the time they got to their hotel—The Lasalle—it was later than usual.

Irving went right to his room to turn in.

"No late-night walks," Clint reminded him.

"I remember," Irving said, and closed the door.

Clint walked Terry to her room, and she pulled him in, not taking no for an answer. He spent the night with her, then went to his own room to dress for breakfast.

He had breakfast in the dining room with Irving and Terry, and they left for the train station, sending their luggage ahead.

* * *

"That went extremely well," Irving said in the dining car. It was too late for breakfast and too early for lunch, so they were having drinks. It was never too early for drinks, Irving said.

"I think we did our best work in Chicago," Ellen Terry said. "Chicago will remember us."

"Yes, they will."

"What's wrong with you?" Terry asked Clint.

"What do you mean?"

"You're looking around so much you're going to hurt your neck."

"I'm doing my job, Ellen," Clint said.

Actually, he was looking around for a waiter again, to try and get a Chicago newspaper. He wanted to see if a girl had been killed during the time they were there.

He didn't know for sure, but Irving claimed he didn't go out. If a girl got killed, it meant one of two things. Either Irving wasn't a killer, or he did go out and lied about it.

"Are we going to go through this again?" Terry asked.

"What?"

"You having to walk the train, look for killers, and not find any."

"Well," Irving said, "I certainly hope the last part is true."

Mr. Gray sat at a table at the other end of the car, nursing a cup of coffee. Mr. Green was in one of the passenger cars. They decided never to be seen together. They'd even sat separately at the theater the night before.

He watched as Adams and the two actors stood up and left the car.

They had about a fifteen-hour trip, so Clint once again got them all compartments. It also kept Irving and Terry away from the general public on the train.

"It's too early to turn in," Irving said. "I'm going to do some reading."

Clint and Terry left Irving at his compartment and walked to hers.

When they got to her door, she said, "Yes, don't tell me. You have work to do." She went into her compartment. "I will see you later." She closed the door.

THIRTY-FOUR

Clint had booked them on the train that arrived in Saint Louis early the next morning. By that time he had met both conductors, and one of them had gotten him copies of the *Chicago Tribune* and the *Chicago Sun*.

He went through both newspapers while Irving and Terry were in their compartments. He didn't find any stories about a girl being killed. He thought that would make him feel better, but it didn't. No murder could have meant that Irving really did stay in his room, which meant that he might not have murdered the girls in those other cities but it didn't prove it.

They collected the luggage and got two cabs to their hotel in Saint Louis, the Mayflower.

"This is beautiful," Terry said as they walked through the lobby.

"I'm trying to get you into the best places," Clint said, "but you better enjoy this one. The further west we get, the less the hotels look like this."

"Well, I for one will enjoy this one thoroughly," Irving said.

They got checked in, and two bellmen helped them carry the luggage up to their rooms. Once again suites for the two actors, but a regular room for Clint.

"What will you be doing today?" Terry asked.

"Keeping you and Henry alive."

"Well, we've arrived so early we have a lot of time before the performance," she said. "I would like to see some of Saint Louis, perhaps sample the local cuisine."

"I don't know if what they have here is called cuisine," Clint said.

"I would also like to try it," Irving said.

"All right," Clint said. "Let's freshen up in our rooms. I'll pick you both up in an hour and we'll go for a walk."

"Excellent," Irving said.

"Don't either of you leave your rooms without me," he said.

"Understood," Irving said.

"Ellen?"

"Fine."

They left Terry in her room and walked to Irving's.

"You should be careful," Irving said as he opened his door.

"I'm always careful."

"No," Irving said, "I mean about Ellen."

"What do you mean about Ellen?"

Irving smiled.

"I notice she's treating you differently," he said. "I think I know why."

"Henry—"

"No, no," Irving said, "that's fine with me. I just want to warn you. Ellen has a history of . . . well, breaking hearts."

"She's not going to break mine," Clint said. "Don't worry about that."

"Well, that's good," Irving said. "Very good."

"I'll see you in an hour," Clint said. Irving closed his door.

Clint went down the hall to his room, entered, took off his gun belt and shirt. He used the pitcher and basin to get cleaned up, then changed into a clean shirt—his last one, he noticed. He didn't travel with chests full of clothing like Irving and Terry did. He was going to have to buy some new shirts, or have the ones he already had washed.

He'd eaten in Saint Louis many times. They had good steaks, but he never thought of the food as cuisine. He wondered how Ellen Terry would react.

It was too early to meet with Irving and Terry, so he went downstairs to the lobby and into the bar.

"Can I get a beer?" he asked the bartender. He looked around, saw that most of the men in the place were drinking coffee at that hour.

"You can get whatever you want, sir," the bartender said. "You're a guest, right?"

"That's right."

"Beer comin' up," the man said, "nice and cold."

The bartender, a young man in a very white shirt with red sleeve garters, set the beer down in front of Clint and smiled.

"Welcome to Saint Louis, sir. The first drink is on the house."

"That's very kind of you, thanks."

He'd eaten in St. Louis many times

"Are you here for business or pleasure?" the man asked.

Clint gave the answer that usually meant you didn't want to talk about it.

"A little of both."

"Gotcha," the man said, taking the hint. "Enjoy."

He walked away, leaving Clint to enjoy his beer.

"I wish we could go in there and have a drink," Mr. Green said.

"Well, we can't," Mr. Gray said. "And we shouldn't even be standing here together." They were right across the street from the Mayflower Hotel. "You stay here and watch."

"Where are you going?"

"To send a telegram," Mr. Gray said, "and to get us a room in a hotel on Laclede's Landing."

"That's the riverfront, isn't it?"

"It is."

"Do we have to stay down there?"

"It's safer," Mr. Gray said. "Adams won't be taking the actors down there."

"Well, yeah, maybe, but—"

"Just stay here and watch," Mr. Gray said. "Follow them if they leave, but don't get noticed."

"I won't," Mr. Green said. "I have done this before, you know."

"I do know," Mr. Gray said. "Just be careful."

"I have been careful since I left New York," Mr. Green said. "And I'm not looking forward to getting any further away from there."

"We'll be crossing the Mississippi after this," Mr. Gray said.

"Jesus—"

"We are going to need some new clothes."

"What's the matter with my suit?"

"It's not what they're wearing in the West these days, Mr. Green," Mr. Gray said. "No, it won't do at all. We'll need to get ourselves some Western garb."

As Mr. Gray walked away, Mr. Green hissed after him, "Well, I'm not wearing spurs!"

THIRTY-FIVE

Clint finished his beer, thanked the bartender again, and then went upstairs to collect his charges. He went to Henry Irving's room first. The actor opened the door, dressed to go out. He wore a three-piece suit, but no hat and walking stick this time.

"Just in time," Irving said. "I'm ready to go."

"Wouldn't you like to dress more casually?" Clint asked.

"This is casual," Irving said. "I am not wearing my cape. After all, I am not a farmer."

"Okay."

Irving closed his door and they walked to Terry's. She opened the door with a smile, but it dimmed when she saw that Irving was with Clint—or that Clint was with Irving.

She was wearing a dress that covered her from neck to ankle, and a shawl over her shoulders. It was certainly more casual than what Irving was wearing, but not exactly casual by local standards.

Clint was wearing his gun and holster. While in the East, and even in Chicago, he had worn the smaller Colt New Line, keeping it hidden from view. Closer to the West, however, he felt more comfortable with his holster on his hip.

"That's what you are wearing?" Terry asked him.

Clint looked down at his shirt—his last clean shirt—and his Levi's and said, "There's nothing wrong with what I'm wearing."

"If you say so," she said. She looked at Irving, who shrugged.

"What would you like to see?" he asked as they walked downstairs.

"The city, Clint," Irving said. "I would like to see the city."

"And sample the food," Terry said. "We have been rushed in every city we've been to. I would like to make use of this extra time and eat somewhere other than the hotel dining room."

"All right," Clint said. "I think I know a good place to eat, but first we'll walk around a bit."

As they stepped outside in front of the hotel, Irving said, "I have heard something about a place called Laclede's Landing."

"That's the riverfront," Clint said. "You don't want to go there."

"No," Terry said, "we certainly do not."

"Why not?" Irving asked.

"It's not a good place to walk," Clint said.

"Like the East End in London, Henry," Ellen Terry said. "You wouldn't go there, would you?"

Irving didn't answer, although he seemed to be considering the question.

Clint took them for a walk around Saint Louis, took them to a spot from which they were able to see the Mississippi, without taking them to the riverfront.

"Is that the riverfront down there?" Irving asked.

"Part of it."

"It doesn't look so bad."

"Maybe not from here," Clint said. "Come on, I know a place near here where we can eat."

As they walked, Terry asked Irving, "Why are you so interested in the riverfront?"

"Oh, I don't know," he said. "Lately I'm just . . . curious about some things."

"Like what?" she asked.

"Like . . . violence."

She looked surprised.

"Why would you be interested in violence?"

"I have experienced so little of it in my life," Irving said.

"How about getting shot at?" Clint asked. "Wasn't that violent enough for you?"

"You see," Irving said, "you would think so, but that just seems to have made me even more interested."

"Interested how?" she asked. "You want to experience it, or inflict it?"

"Inflict it?" He looked interested. "That thought had never occurred to me. I've thought about . . . watching it."

"What about a boxing match?" Clint asked.

"That is controlled violence. I find myself being curious about more uncontrolled violence. Perhaps even frenzied."

"Well," Clint said, "the riverfront would probably be the place to go, but I wouldn't go there alone."

"Would you take me there?"

"There's our restaurant up ahead," Clint said. "Let's talk about it once we're seated."

THIRTY-SIX

The restaurant was called Blondie's. Clint had eaten there a time or two before on his trips to Saint Louis. He remembered they had great steaks, stew, and desserts. And they had something he really couldn't get anywhere else—pork steaks. That seemed to be a Saint Louis specialty.

Irving agreed to try a pork steak, so he and Clint both ordered it. Ellen Terry opted for the beef stew.

"Now can we talk about the riverfront?" Irving asked Clint.

"Henry," Clint said, "these walks you like to take at night . . . is that what it's all about. Trying to find, to observe violence?"

"I suppose so," Irving said.

"I don't understand, Henry," Ellen Terry said. "You're a gentle, talented man."

"I am a boring man, Ellen," Irving said. He looked

at Clint. "Look at you. Violence is an integral part of your life. Do you have a boring life?"

"No, I don't," Clint said, "and sometimes I wish I did."

"Why?" the actor asked.

"Henry," Clint said, "somebody tries to kill me a dozen times a year, maybe more."

"But . . . why?"

"Because of who I am," Clint said. "And I don't like it. But I'm stuck with a life of violence. Why would you want to go looking for it?"

"Because I haven't experienced it, except on stage," Irving said. "I think it would add nuances to my performance that I've never achieved before."

"I don't agree, Henry," Terry said. "I think your nuances are just fine the way they are."

The waitress brought their lunches, smiled at Clint, and asked, "Do you need anything else, honey?"

She was in her thirties, built solidly, with black hair and pale skin. Her eyes were an odd color, almost purple in hue.

"I'd like a beer," he said.

"I would like one as well," Irving said.

"Comin' right up," she said. "What about you, sweetie?"

"Do you have a wine list?" Terry asked.

"I'm afraid not, Duchess," the waitress said. "This ain't that kind of place."

"Just bring her a glass of whatever wine you have," Clint said.

"Sure thing."

She walked away, twitching her hips for Clint's benefit.

"What an attractive girl," Irving said.

"In a cheap sort of way," Terry said.

They ate, talked about places they'd been, places they were going to. Clint thought Irving might have forgotten about his quest for violence.

". . . and before we go to San Francisco," Irving finished saying, "we're going to Tombstone to play the famous Birdcage Theater."

"The Birdcage," Clint said, surprised. "Henry. That place isn't what it used to be—and neither is Tombstone."

"But it is one of the most famous theaters in your country, isn't it?" Irving asked.

"That may be true," Clint said, "but it's fallen on hard times."

"Well," Irving said, "maybe Ellen and I can bring it back to its former glory."

THIRTY-SEVEN

Mr. Gray waited outside the telegraph office for his reply, which he was certain would come almost immediately. He was right.

"Hey, mister," the clerk called out. "Here's your answer."

Mr. Gray went back inside.

"Thanks." He took the telegram from the clerk, stepped outside to read it.

DO WHAT MUST BE DONE

The telegram was unsigned, but he knew whom it was from.

He folded the telegram, put it in his pocket, and went to find Mr. Green again.

When Clint Adams left the restaurant with Henry Irving and Ellen Terry, Mr. Green followed at a discreet distance. They seemed to simply be walking around the city. But eventually, they headed back to their hotel, and Mr. Green followed. He found Mr. Gray waiting there for him.

Clint, Irving, and Terry went into the hotel. Mr. Gray and Mr. Green came together across the street.

"Plans have changed," Mr. Gray said.

"What do you mean?" Mr. Green asked.

"They want us to do the job now."

"What?"

"No more waiting."

"I thought they wanted some Western gunman to do the job," Mr. Green said.

"Well," Mr. Gray said, "now it's to be us."

"When?"

"As soon as possible."

"Then . . . tonight? Before the performance?"

"After, I think."

"But—"

"It would be easier to do it after. There would be less likelihood of having to run afterward."

"How will we do it?"

Mr. Gray took his gun from his shoulder holster and said, "We will do it the easy way."

"That's the easy way?"

Mr. Gray knew that Mr. Green had a similar gun underneath his own arm. He also knew that Mr. Green had not yet ever killed anyone.

"Don't worry," he said to his colleague. "It'll be easy."

THIRTY-EIGHT

Clint detected a difference in the Saint Louis audience that made him think the farther west they went, the harder it was going to get for Irving and Terry to command those standing ovations.

"What was wrong with them?" Terry asked on the way back to the hotel.

"Obviously, they didn't like us, Ellen."

"I realize that," she said, "but why?"

They both looked to Clint for an answer.

"It's the West," he said. "It's a different way of life out here."

"This is the West?" Terry asked.

Clint pointed to the Mississippi and said, "On the other side—but this is close."

"Then what is going to happen," she asked, "when we get to the other side?"

"When we get there," Henry Irving said, "we'll win them over, my dear. Don't worry."

When they reached the hotel, Irving and Terry went to their respective suites.

"You want me to come in?" Clint asked Terry.

"Not tonight, Clint," Terry said. "I am not used to the kind of reception we got tonight. I have some thinking to do."

She kissed him on the cheek and left him standing out in the hall.

Clint went down to the lobby, thought about getting a drink somewhere, but then he saw the two men. He recognized one of them. At least, he thought he had seen the man in the back of one of the theaters—probably in Philadelphia.

If this man, and the other one with him, had been following them since then, Clint thought he must be losing it. Either that or he was way too involved with Irving and Terry's comfort than he was with their welfare.

He stepped to the side of the lobby, against a wall, so he could watch them walk by without their seeing him. They went up the stairs leading from the lobby to the second floor. Clint looked around the lobby. People were milling about, paying no attention to him, or to them.

He considered his options. If he waited in the lobby for them to come down, it was possible they would have already killed Henry Irving and left him in his room. It would have been easier to take them in the lobby, where there was more room, but he couldn't risk their killing Irving right in his own room.

He rushed across the lobby and up the stairs.

* * *

Henry Irving answered the knock on his door, expecting to see Clint Adams. What he saw were two men in expensive suits, holding guns.

"Gentlemen."

"You're coming with us, sir," Mr. Gray said.

"My word," Irving said. "Polite gunmen?"

"Mr. Irving," Mr. Gray said, "please don't give us any trouble."

"Well, why not?" Irving asked. "If I let you take me out of this hotel, you will kill me, won't you?"

Mr. Green looked at Mr. Gray, who could feel his colleague staring at him, but didn't return the look.

"We could kill him here," Mr. Green said.

"Too much noise," Mr. Gray said. "But if he forces us into it—"

"Gentlemen," Irving said, "this is fascinating. Please, continue."

At that point the door to Ellen Terry's room opened and she stepped out. When she saw the men in front of Irving's door, she yelled, "What are you doing there?"

Mr. Gray said to Mr. Green, "Get her!"

"Kill her?" Mr. Green asked.

"No," Mr. Gray said, "just get her."

Mr. Green nodded, turned to run down the hall after Ellen Terry. At that moment Clint Adams appeared at the far end of the hall.

"Ellen! Get back inside!" he shouted.

As an actress who had been taking direction for years, she never hesitated. She turned and ran back into her room, slamming and locking the door behind her.

* * *

When the door slammed, Clint looked down the hall at the two gunmen. One had started down the hall toward Terry, while the other remained in front of Henry Irving's door. They both had guns in their hands.

"Step away from the door," Clint said.

He waited for the two men to react, not wanting to shoot if he didn't have to.

Mr. Gray looked at Irving, who hadn't moved. All he had to do was pull the trigger, but then there would be the Gunsmith to deal with.

Instead of shooting, he reached out, grabbed the front of Irving's shirt, and pulled him into the hall.

"Mr. Green!" he said. "Kill him!"

"Wha—"

Mr. Green overcame his split second of surprise another split second too slow. He raised his gun to point it at Clint Adams, but knew he was too late.

At least he never had to wear spurs!

Clint drew quickly, even as Mr. Green was pointing his gun. He fired once. The bullet hit Mr. Green in the chest. It was as if his feet were nailed to the floor. He didn't stagger back or forward, he just crumpled to the floor, his gun landing a second later.

Mr. Gray watched Mr. Green hit the floor, and pulled Irving in front of him. He pointed his gun down the hall at Clint.

"Drop it!" he shouted.

"Not a chance," Clint said.

Mr. Gray put the gun to Henry Irving's temple.

"I'll blow his head off."

"Then you're a dead man," Clint said, "with no shield."

"We're walking out of here."

"Not with him, you're not," Clint said. "He still has a tour to finish."

"You might stop me," Mr. Gray said, "you might even kill me, but there will be others. Lots of others."

"But . . . why?" Irving asked.

"Shut up!" Mr. Gray said, screwing the gun barrel tighter against Irving's head. He never took his eyes off Clint. "Now, drop your gun and step aside."

Clint shook his head.

"Can't do that, friend."

"Then the actor dies."

"Clint," Henry Irving said, "I don't mind dying on stage every so often. That happens to actors. But this . . ."

"Don't worry, Henry," Clint said. "You're not going to die."

Clint had one shot. Irving was a bigger man than the gunman standing behind him, but in order to see Clint, the man still had to look over Irving's shoulder, which left his head exposed. Plus, he had Irving bent backward, which made the actor shorter than he really was.

"Relax, Henry," Clint said. "Don't move."

"W-What are you going to do?" Irving asked, and Mr. Gray wondered the same thing.

Clint fired once, pointing, not aiming. The bullet traveled straight and true, and hit Mr. Gray in his left eye. The bullet went straight through, and out the back of his head.

Irving felt the arm around his neck relax, and he darted away as the man fell to the floor. Spread out on the floor behind them were the man's brains.

"Oh, my," Irving said.

Clint walked up next to him and asked, "Is that enough violence for you?"

THIRTY-NINE

Ellen Terry opened the door to her room and stepped out.

"Is everything all right?" she asked.

"There are two dead men in the hallway, my dear," Irving said. "And they are dead instead of me, thanks to Clint. So I would say everything is as it should be."

Clint had checked the two bodies to make sure they were dead, then replaced the empty loads in his gun with full ones. He holstered the gun and walked over to Terry.

"It's fine," he said. "Just stay inside. There will probably be some law here soon. I'll talk to them."

"They tried to kill Henry?"

"They tried to take him," Clint said. "I assume they would have killed him when they got him away from here."

"And then?" she asked. "Would they have come for me?"

"Probably."

"Oh, God."

Clint put his hand on her shoulder.

"It's fine now," he said. "Go back inside."

"But . . . what if someone else comes?"

"If they do, it won't be tonight," Clint assured her.

She nodded, walked back into her room as if she were in a trance. Clint closed the door behind her, then turned to face Irving. He found the actor still looking down at the two dead men.

"Henry, you have to go back into your room," he said.

Irving turned and asked, "Why? When the local constabulary arrives, I should talk to them. After all, this was all about me."

"If they want to talk to you, they'll knock on your door."

"After what happened," Irving said, "I am not sure I would open it."

"Okay," Clint said, "so leave your door open."

At that moment they heard running footsteps coming up the steps.

"Here they come," Clint said.

"Who?" Irving asked.

"Somebody," Clint replied, "and they're in a hurry. Go on, get inside."

This time Henry Irving obeyed without question, but he did leave his door open.

Clint looked down the hall in time to see three men come running in. They stopped short when they saw him, and the bodies. Clint didn't see any badges.

"Can I help you boys?" he asked.

They were all wearing dark suits, and the one in front

pulled his jacket aside. Clint saw a gun in a shoulder rig, and a badge pinned to his vest.

"We're the law, fella," the man said. "Saint Louis Police Department."

The other three also moved their jackets aside to show their badges. The spokesman was in his thirties; the other two looked younger.

"No sheriff?" Clint asked.

"He might be along, too," the man said. "We beat him to it. What happened here?"

"These two tried to kidnap a man," Clint said. "I stopped them."

"Kidnap who?"

"A man named Henry Irving."

"Who's that?" one of them asked.

"Don't you read the papers?" the other asked. "He's some visiting actor."

"He's a famous actor from England," the first man said. He looked at Clint. "I was at the theater tonight. Is he all right?"

"He's okay," Clint said. "He's in his room, if you need to talk to him."

"Guess we better," the man said.

The three men came down the hall, stepped around Mr. Green's body. They stopped by Clint, looked down at Mr. Gray.

"Gonna be hell gettin' that out of the rug," one of them said.

"What's your name, mister?" the first man asked.

"Clint Adams."

The man looked surprised.

"The Gunsmith, right?"

"That's right."

"I'm Officer Chantry," the man said. "What's your connection?"

"I'm the escort for Henry Irving and Ellen Terry."

"Escort, or bodyguard?" one of the others asked.

"Both."

Chantry turned to the others.

"You two stay out here. I'll talk to Mr. Irving."

"What are we supposed to do?" one of them asked.

"Billy, you stay here. Eddie, get somebody to help remove these bodies."

"Yeah, okay," Eddie said.

Chantry turned back to Clint.

"The lady okay?"

"She's fine. In her room. Mr. Irving's in here."

Clint led Chantry to Irving's door, and they entered. The actor was sitting in a chair with a glass of brandy.

FORTY

"Henry, this is Officer Chantry, of the Saint Louis Police Department."

"Mr. Henry," Office Chantry said. "I was in the Fox Theater to see you tonight. I thought you and the lady were great."

"Did you?" Irving displayed some surprise. "Seems you were in the minority."

"Aw, don't let them get you down," Chantry said. "This town don't know nothing about acting. You and the lady deserved better."

"Apparently not," Irving said. "Those two out in the hall were harsh critics."

"Can you tell me what happened here tonight?" Chantry asked.

"Those two men came to my door with their guns and tried to take me out," Irving said. "I believe they wanted to kill me." He indicated Clint with his brandy glass. "Mr. Adams stopped them."

Chantry turned to Clint.

"That all?"

"That's it."

"This something that's been going on?"

"They were tailing us," Clint said. "Looks like they finally decided to make a move."

"Well," Chantry said, "sounds like self-defense to me. I'll explain it to my chief."

"Would you like a glass of brandy, Officer?" Irving asked.

"Sure, why not?" Chantry said. "Looks like I'll be up here for a while. At least until we get those bodies cleared away."

"Clint?"

"I'm going to go and check on Ellen," Clint said. "Make sure she's all right. The officer will stay with you."

"Don't leave the hotel, Mr. Adams." Chantry said. "Not yet."

"I'm not leaving," Clint said.

While Irving poured the officer a glass of brandy and handed it to him, Clint left the room, walked down the hall past the other policeman to Terry's door, and knocked.

"Clint," Terry said when she opened the door.

"Can I come in?"

"Please."

She backed away. He entered the room. She rushed into his arms.

"Is it over?"

"For now," he said.

"Will it happen again?"

"Maybe," Clint said. "I can't say for sure."

"Who were they?"

"I don't know," Clint said. "I wish I'd been able to take one of them alive to find out, but I guess that wasn't to be."

"So what do we do now?" she asked, stepping back.

"I'll wait until the police search them," Clint said, "find out who they are, where they were from."

"And then what?"

"Then we continue in," Clint said. "Kansas City's next."

"Will we be late?"

"If we are," Clint said, "they'll wait. After all, they can't start without you and Henry, can they?"

FORTY-ONE

Kansas City went only slightly worse than Saint Louis, except that no one tried to kidnap or kill Irving or Ellen Terry. But their reception in Saint Louis and Kansas City had Clint worried about what they'd find in Tombstone, which would be their stop before Phoenix and then San Francisco.

The night before they were to leave for Tombstone—by rail, and then by stage from Benson—they had dinner in Henry Irving's suite. The hotel brought up a table and supplied two waiters for the meal.

"I don't mind telling you," Ellen Terry said to them both, "I've been very nervous since Saint Louis."

"You've been nervous?" Irving said. "I have never been as drunk as I was that night after it was all over. I don't even remember getting on the train the next morning."

"Well, you did," Clint said, and to Terry, he said,

"Don't be nervous. I think we gave them something to think about in Saint Louis."

"We gave them something to think about?" she asked. "You mean *you* did."

"Jesus," she said, "I just thought of something."

"What's that, my dear?" Irving asked.

"We are going to Tombstone next."

"So?"

"That is the Wild West," she said to him. "There will be more guns there than anywhere else."

Irving looked at Clint.

"I guess I can't argue with her on any of that," he told the actor.

"If they don't like us on stage," she went on, "they might shoot us."

"I doubt that," Irving said, "but you are right about one thing."

"Oh? And what's that?" she asked.

"It will probably be the most dangerous place we've been."

"And how do you feel about that?" she asked.

"I think," Irving continued, "that given all the places we've already been, Tombstone is where Clint will be the most comfortable."

Now Ellen Terry looked at Clint, and he shrugged and said, "I can't argue with him either."

"And you think you can keep us safe there?" she asked him.

"I believe I can," Clint said, "but maybe I'll send a couple of telegrams before we leave here, just in case."

"To whom?" she asked.

"Not important." He leaned over, took a metal cover off a plate, to reveal a chocolate cake. "Anyone for cake?"

Clint walked Terry to her suite and promised to join her later. Then he went back to Irving's.

"I'll have somebody come and clean up," he said.

"They can do that tomorrow, after we leave," Irving said. "Have a drink with me."

The actor poured two brandies, handed Clint one.

"What's on your mind?" Clint asked.

"Violence." Irving sat in a stuffed armchair. Clint sat on a wooden chair.

"You haven't had enough of it?"

"I won't pretend I wasn't frightened," Irving said. "And, in fact, I still am. But I'm afraid I am even more fascinated."

"What do you want to do, Henry?" Clint asked. "Where do you want to go now?"

"I think we are already going there," Irving said. "Tombstone is a dangerous place. It has seen much violence."

"So have Dodge City, Abilene, Deadwood," Clint said. "But they all have one thing in common."

"What is that?"

"Their most violent days are in the past."

"I see."

They sipped their drinks for a few minutes, then Clint asked, "Do you want me to find you someplace that's still violent?"

Irving smiled.

"Not necessary," he said. "I think violence is

everywhere. If I really wanted to find it, I don't think I would have much trouble."

"Probably not, but after Saint Louis—"

"You would think I wouldn't want any part of it, is that it?"

"Well," Clint said, "you *were* almost killed."

"Yes, I was," Irving said. "Tell me, what was it like?"

"What was what like?"

"Killing those men?" Irving asked. "How did it feel?"

"Why do you want to know that?" Clint asked.

"Many of the characters I play have killed people," Irving said. "I would just like to know how to play them better."

"It doesn't feel good, Henry," Clint said. "It doesn't feel good at all."

"Then why do you do it?"

"I only do it when I have to," Clint said. "To stay alive."

"And keep others alive?"

"Sometimes."

"And when you save someone's life, doesn't that feel good?"

"It does, but the killing . . ." Clint shook his head. "Never."

"Well," Irving said, "I suppose I will have to take your word for that."

"I hope you do."

"What about those dead girls?" Irving asked.

"What about them?"

"Were there any in Saint Louis?"

"I don't know, Henry," Clint said. "I didn't check."

"I was just curious."

Clint put his brandy glass down, still half full, and stood up.

"I'm going to turn in," he said. "Tomorrow we head for Tombstone."

Irving got up and walked Clint to the door, his arm around Clint's shoulders.

"I'm looking forward to it, Clint," he said. "Looking forward to it."

FORTY-TWO

Tombstone, Arizona

There were no dead girls in Saint Louis. At least, not the night Clint was there with Irving and Ellen Terry. He found that out the next morning, when he was sending telegrams.

When the stage from Benson pulled into Tombstone, Clint got out, turned to help Ellen Terry down. It was early afternoon, and they were not to perform until the next evening.

"Oh, my God," she said. "Is it over? Are we here?"

"We're here, Ellen."

"Thank God."

Henry Irving stepped down, began slapping dust from his suit.

"Mr. Adams?"

Clint turned, saw a man with a badge approaching him. There was another man behind him, wearing a dark suit.

"I'm Marshal Cuthbert," he said, putting his hand out. "This is Mayor Danvers."

Clint shook hands with both of them, and said, "This is Henry Irving, and Ellen Terry."

"Sir, ma'am," the mayor said to them, executing a slight bow from the waist, "we're honored to have you playing the Birdcage."

"We're honored to be here, Mayor," Irving said. "Aren't we, Ellen?"

"Oh, yes," Terry said, "honored. Where is our hotel?"

"Why, right here," the mayor said. "We had the stage stop right in front of the Palace Hotel."

Terry looked at the two-story wooden building in front of her and asked, "This is it?"

"Yes, ma'am," the marshal said, "this is it."

"Marshal," Clint said, "I'll take Mr. Irving and Miss Terry to their rooms. Can you have some men bring their baggage?"

"Sure thing," the marshal said.

"We'd, uh, like to have supper with our guests later this evening," the mayor said to Clint. "At Delmonico's? Uh, you, too, Mr. Adams."

"What time?" Clint asked.

"Oh . . . is six okay?"

"We'll be there, Mr. Mayor," Clint said. "Thanks you."

Clint escorted the actors into the hotel.

There was only one suite, so they gave it to Ellen Terry. Henry Irving got a large room, Clint a small one.

"You can freshen up and wait here for me," he told both of them. "The mayor wants us to go to supper with him."

"Where are you going?" Terry asked.

"I'm going to check for telegrams," Clint said. "I'll be back to pick you up."

"All right."

"And Henry."

"Yes?"

"This is not the town to go walking in."

"I thought you said it wasn't violent," Irving asked.

"I said it's most violent days were behind it," Clint said. "That doesn't mean you still couldn't get yourself killed."

"I will make sure he stays inside, Clint."

"Good."

Tombstone had changed quite a bit since its boom days. Clint had been there a couple years ago, and it hadn't grown much since then, but it had changed quite a bit since the Earp days.

He walked to where the telegraph office used to be and it was still there. He went inside and asked if there were any telegrams for him.

"Got two here for ya, Mr. Adams," the young clerk said.

"Thank you."

The young man handed him the telegrams and said, "I heard you was here when the Earps were. Is that true?"

"No time for stories now, son," Clint said. "Thanks."

He stepped outside and read the telegrams. He'd been hoping to find Bat Masterson in the vicinity, but one telegram told him that wasn't to be. So he was going to have to protect Irving and Terry himself while they were in Tombstone—unless he ran into somebody he knew.

The other telegram was from Washington. Trehearn had followed up on the two men Clint had killed in Saint Louis. They were from New York, identified only by code names. Agents had been dispatched there, and arrests had been made. But he warned Clint that others might already have been hired to keep pursuing the actors.

That wasn't good news. Chances were good it wouldn't be a couple of New York thugs who would come after them this time. Chances were good it would be two or three guns who knew what they were doing.

He headed back to the hotel.

FORTY-THREE

They all had steaks at Delmonico's, even Ellen Terry. Turned out the mayor was a big Shakespeare fan, talked with Henry Irving all evening about different plays. The marshal was there, eating and looking bored. Every so often, though, he'd throw a look Ellen Terry's way.

Clint leaned over, as the man was sitting right next to him.

"Beautiful, isn't she?" he asked the marshal.

"Huh? Oh, yeah, she sure is."

"You want to keep her alive?"

"Huh?"

"Somebody's liable to try to kill one of them, or both, while we're here," Clint said.

"What? Why?"

"They tried in Saint Louis," Clint said. "I'm not sure why. Some kind of conspiracy, it seems, perhaps to start an international incident between the two countries."

"What happened?"

"The gunmen weren't good enough," Clint said, "but out here, I think they'll send somebody better."

"Whataya want me to do?"

"You got deputies?"

"Two."

"Place them in the back of the theater," Clint said.

"What about the hotel?"

"I'll be in the hotel with them all night," Clint said. "If you want, you can put one of your men in the lobby. But I'm worried about the Birdcage."

"Okay," Marshal Cuthbert said. "My boys'll be there and so will I. Where will you be?"

"Backstage."

Cuthbert nodded and the mayor called for the check.

Clint did something that night he hadn't done in any of the other cities. Instead of spending the night in his room, or Terry's, he spent it out in the hallway, sitting up in a chair. That way nobody could get into their rooms, and Henry Irving couldn't get out.

Clint didn't like all of Irving's talk about violence. The man was just too damn fascinated by it, and it started Clint thinking about all the dead girls again. So he didn't want Henry Irving taking any late-night walks.

FORTY-FOUR

The Birdcage hadn't changed much, except for the fact that Doc Holliday wasn't at his usual faro table. Clint also noticed that the whores had been given the night off.

They had remained in their hotel rooms all day, and Clint had stayed in the building. The marshal had his deputies take turns in the hallway. They had kept them safe all day, and then they all accompanied them to the theater.

The audience wasn't large, but they seemed appreciative of Irving and Terry's readings. Or maybe they were just taking their cue from the mayor, who applauded wildly after each one.

From his position backstage, Clint could see the marshal in the front with the mayor, and the two deputies in the back. This was the smallest theater the actors had played in the United States, but the one with the most history.

They finished their readings, took their bows, and came offstage in Clint's direction. The audience kept applauding.

"They liked us," Terry said to Clint.

"Of course they did."

"We should do an encore," Irving said.

"No," Clint said. "Don't press your luck."

"You're right, of course," Irving said. "They might not like it."

"I meant nobody shot at you tonight," Clint said. "Let's not press our luck."

There were two men watching from the audience, not seated together. They each had a job to do. Evan Horn had the job of killing Henry Irving and Ellen Terry. He didn't know why, and he didn't care. He'd been told that if he could get only one, get the man. But watching the woman onstage, he wanted to get his hands on her.

The other man's name was Joe Kendall. He was a fast gun, had more than a dozen kills to his credit in fair fights. He was going after the Gunsmith. And he had no doubt that he'd get him.

They applauded along with the rest of the crowd, and then filed out with them.

The marshal came up on the stage and joined Clint in the wings.

"Where are your men?" Clint asked.

"Breaking up fights out front," Cuthbert said. "Where are Mr. Irving and Miss Terry?"

"In their dressing rooms, getting ready to go back to the hotel."

"The mayor wants to eat with them again," the marshal said. "Said he's waiting out front."

"Okay," Clint said. "I'll tell them. Let's wait for the fights to stop and everyone to head home."

"I'll go out front and make sure it's clear for you to bring them out."

"Good, thanks."

As the marshal went back onto the stage and made his way out of the Birdcage, Clint walked to the dressing rooms. He knocked on Irving's door.

"The mayor wants to buy supper again," he said as Irving opened his door.

"That's fine," Irving said. "Let's get Ellen and go."

They knocked on Terry's door, then knocked again. Clint started to get worried when the door opened.

"You're very impatient," she said. "Are we going to eat?"

"With the mayor again," Irving said.

"Oh, that boring man?"

"It's his town," Irving said, "and he's buying supper."

"Steak again?" she asked.

"You can order anything you want," Clint said.

"Then let's go," she said. "I'm starved."

They walked to the front of the theater and stepped outside. The only person there was the marshal.

"The others are gone," Cuthbert said. "The mayor's waiting—"

There was a shot and the marshal staggered, looked surprised, and fell to the ground.

Clint drew his gun, stepped in front of Irving, and pulled Terry behind him.

"Where did that come from?" Irving asked.

"I don't know," Clint said. He studied the buildings across the street, the rooftops, the shaded doorways. It was dark already, and there wasn't much of a moon. The streetlights were feeble at best.

"Stay behind me." Clint said, "and back up to the front of the theater."

They got to the door, but when Irving tried it, it was locked.

"Now what?" Irving asked.

"We wait."

"What do we do now?" Horn asked.

"This is Tombstone, Evan," Kendall said. "What do you think we do?"

Horn looked at his colleague and said, "O.K. Corral?"

"No, stupid," Kendall said, "right here, on the street. The Tombstone way."

"But that's the Gunsmith."

"You do your job," Kendall said, "and I'll do mine."

"Adams!" a voice called out. "Holster your gun."

Clint stared across the street, but it was too dark.

"Come on out," he called back.

"Holster it, and we'll step out."

"Clint, don't," Terry said.

"Just stay here," Clint said. "In the dark. Henry, keep her here in the doorway."

Irving put his arm around Terry.

Clint holstered his gun and stepped into the street.

Two men stepped out into the meager light, one slightly behind the other. Clint thought he knew what they had in mind. The first man would kill him, and then the other one would take care of Irving and Ellen Terry.

They both had their guns holstered. Clint marveled at the ego of some men—most men.

"This isn't a good idea," he said.

"My name's Kendall," the first man said, "Joe Kendall. You know it?"

"Never heard of you."

"Well, you have now," Kendall said. "And after tonight, so will everyone else."

"Your friend better draw, too," Clint said, "because I'm going to kill both of you."

"Hey, wait—" Horn said.

But Kendall didn't wait. He sealed both their fates by drawing his gun.

"Clint!" Ellen Terry's voice called out.

Clint drew his gun, shot the first man in the chest. Kendall was shocked. He never got his gun out of his holster. It was still there when he hit the ground.

Horn grabbed for his gun, but in his haste he shoved it deeper into his holster before trying to pull it out. He died that way, with his hand on his gun.

Clint walked to both men, checked to make sure they were dead.

Irving and Terry rushed to the fallen lawman. Clint joined them there. He was dead, shot in the back. Suddenly, there was the sound of running, and they were joined by a crowd, including the mayor, and the two deputies.

"What happened?" the mayor asked.

"Let's get off the street, Mr. Mayor," Clint said, "and I'll explain."

FORTY-FIVE

SAN FRANCISCO

Clint got out of the carriage, turned to assist Ellen Terry down. Henry Irving had climbed out the other side. He walked around and joined them.

"The luggage should be on board," he told them.

"Won't you reconsider and come with us?" Ellen Terry asked.

"No," Clint said. "I've seen enough of New York, and the East, to last me awhile."

Their performances in San Francisco had been a triumph, and now they were returning to New York to catch the boat back to England.

"But what if we're still in danger?" Terry asked.

"The conspirators have all been arrested—or killed," Clint said. "They were a group of fanatics who called themselves the Color Guard, with names like Mr. Green and Mr. Blue. They had nothing against you personally—just your country, for reasons only they understood. They tried to hurt your nation by destroying its national treasures."

"How flattering to have been the focus of such intrigue," Irving commented wryly. "But I've played many deranged individuals in my career—tragic heroes whose passion turns to madness. And what about you, Clint, and your fraternity of the gun? I presume you and your colleagues have faced many madmen."

"Of course," Clint replied. "There are madmen everywhere."

"I cannot wait to leave this barbaric land," Ellen said. "What if there are others who wish to harm us, Clint? Who will protect us on our trip back to New York?"

"The United States government has someone waiting for you on the train. His name is Jim West. You can trust him," Clint assured her. "He's a good friend of mine."

Irving put his hand out to the Gunsmith.

"Thank you for everything." They shook hands.

Ellen Terry wrapped her arms around Clint and kissed him soundly on the lips.

"Good-bye, Clint Adams."

"Good-bye, Miss Terry."

He watched them board the train, and watched it pull out of the station. Then he turned and walked back to the carriage.

"Portsmouth Square," he told the driver. "Time for some gambling."

Some years later, when news of Jack the Ripper reached the United States, Clint Adams wondered. Wondered about Henry Irving's late-night walks. And his interest in violence.

He wondered for a long time.

Watch for

THE TOWN OF TWO WOMEN

371st novel in the exciting GUNSMITH series
from Jove

Coming in November!